Praise for The Woman Who Fed the Dogs

'Kristien Hemmerechts didn't write an apology for an inhuman woman, but simply a very good no[illegible]
De Volkskrant

'As is the case with the best wr[illegible] what is said, but what is not sai[illegible] so accomplished'
For Books' Sake

'The narrative is impossible for the reader to escape, unknowingly and at most points unwillingly, you are dragged into her world'
Exeposé

'The naturalness of this reconstruction of a life is mind-blowing'
PANTHEON BOEKHANDEL

'With unnerving conviction, this novel inhabits the mind, heart and voice of Belgium's 'most hated woman', the ex-wife of murderer Marc Dutroux – the authenticity makes for a compelling narrative'
BLAKE MORRISON

'*The Woman Who Fed the Dogs* is a deconstruction of identity. Without sympathising or showing understanding for Martin (Odette), Hemmerechts shows us the inner workings of the mind of a woman with a horrific past and an uncertain future'
Flanders Today

‘Hemmerechts expertly shows us that nothing is simple or black and white: she writes superbly’
We Love This Book

‘As clear as crystal and very impressive’
KNACK

‘A daring, but successful endeavor to paint a probing psychological portrait of a complex personality; astonishing and sometimes provocative in all its directness’
Flanders Literature

‘Raises interesting questions about fear, dependence, guilt, penance and the problem of forgiveness’
Tzum

‘Hemmerechts expertly portrays the connections between sex and power and violence, and how those interact with racism. She also writes superbly about how our childhood forms us as adults’
We Love This Book

‘With this book Hemmerechts has created a very strong thinking exercise with an ingeniously developed main character. All this in a smooth style, which makes the book read like a train’
Hebban

‘Thematically, this story fits seamlessly inside an oeuvre in which parents and children, and in particular women trying to determine their position in relation to others (wherein power and sexuality are recurring motifs), occupy a central place’
Hanta

‘As a psychological novel, the book convinces’
De Leesclub van Alles

‘It grabs you by the throat and doesn’t let you go’
Nine Sisters

‘This penetrating portrait will haunt you long after reading, and throws up more questions than answers, as all good literature should’
NBD BIBLION

KRISTIEN HEMMERECHTS' extensive output includes more than twenty novels, and numerous collections of short stories and autobiographical essays; a body of work that has frequently been praised by critics and awarded prizes. Never one to shy away from controversy, Hemmerechts is known for her forthright opinions on social issues. She used to teach English Literature at University College Brussels and now teaches Creative Writing at the Catholic University of Leuven and The Drama School of Antwerp. She has been awarded the Flemish State Prize and the Frans Kellendonk Prize for her oeuvre.

PAUL VINCENT (UK), Honorary Senior Lecturer in Dutch at UCL, has been one of the most renowned translators of Dutch literature for the past twenty years. He was awarded the first David Reid Poetry Translation Prize (2006) for his translation of 'Herinnering aan Holland' ('Memory of Holland') by Hendrik Marsman and the Vondel Translation Prize 2012 for *My Little War* by Louis Paul Boon. His recent translations include *The Hidden Force* by Louis Couperus, *While the Gods Were Sleeping* by Erwin Mortier, short-listed for the Independent Foreign Fiction Prize, and (with John Irons) *100 Dutch-Language Poems: From the Medieval Period to the Present Day*, joint winner of the Oxford-Weidenfeld Prize 2016.

Kristien Hemmerechts

the Woman who Fed the Dogs

Translated from the Dutch
by Paul Vincent

WORLD EDITIONS
New York, London, Amsterdam

Published in the USA in 2019 by World Editions LLC, New York
Published in the UK in 2015 by World Editions LTD, London

World Editions
New York/London/Amsterdam

Printed by Sheridan, Chelsea, MI, USA

Library of Congress Cataloging in Publication Data is available

ISBN 978-1-64286-007-8

First published as *De Vrouw die de Honden Eten Gaf* in the Netherlands in 2014 by De Geus

The translation of this book is funded by the Flemish Literature Fund (Vlaams Fonds voor de Letteren – www.flemishliterature.be)

Twitter: @WorldEdBooks
Facebook: WorldEditionsInternationalPublishing
www.worldeditions.org

‘The sad truth is that most evil is done by people who never make up their minds to be good or evil.’

HANNAH ARENDT, *The Life of the Mind* (1978)

1

The most hated woman in Belgium. That's what they call me. Much more hated than that woman who murdered her five children. Most people have already forgotten her. Not me. Meanwhile other mothers have murdered their children, though not as resolutely as her, not as unerringly. She is and will remain the queen among murderess-mothers, the gold medallist, the Medea of our age.

I don't deserve a medal. I deserve hatred, scorn, poison. People send me letters in which they describe in great detail what they would do to me if they had the chance. A long, lingering death under torture is what I deserve. Starvation. They enclose photos of emaciated Jews. 'This is what you've got coming the moment you set foot out of prison!'

Don't read them, says Anouk, and Sister Virginie also urges me not to. Ignore them, especially now. Save your strength for the day when you are released, the day they say is fast approaching, to the rage and frustration of the whole country. I must think of the good things, the good things Anouk wants for me and Sister

Virginie also wants for me. Dear, faithful Sister Virginie, who in this hell takes pity on me like a mother, following the example of the Virgin Mary, Refuge of Sinners, Comfortress of the Afflicted. And she also took pity on my Mummy—God rest her soul. It was her idea that I should ask Mummy to pray at her house every day at eight-thirty in the evening. At the same moment I prayed in my cell, and so we were united in prayer. Poor Mummy, who was taken from us far too early. It is always too early, says Sister Virginie, for those we love. How lucky I am to have her, poor orphan, abandoned by everyone, except by her and by God. I do not always feel Him. Forgive me.

And forgive me for reading everything.

M also reads everything that appears about him in the press. So I read in the paper. He cuts it out and puts it in a folder, like me. He will notice that recently more has been written about me than about him. A lot more. It will make him furious. Seething with rage.

Soon I'll be free and you won't, M.

This time I shan't come and visit you. I shan't sit opposite you. I shan't listen to what you've got to say. The jobs you've got for me, the role you've devised for me. I shan't even think about you.

'You owe everything to me. Without me you'd be nothing.'

And I believed him.

I have a poor self-image, says psychotherapist Anouk. That's why I'm an easy prey for bad men. *Was* an easy prey for bad men.

I don't want to hear another word about him. Other things concern me now, such as the question: why are murderess-mothers not hated?

On that subject I don't want to miss a single word. Unfortunately those words dry up in the blink of an eye. You have to be as quick as lightning, and I'm not as quick as lightning, I never have been. Even the champion Geneviève Lhermitte scarcely gets the ink flowing anymore. At the beginning you couldn't turn on the television without there being a news item about her. In every tree in the country a bird chirped her name: Lhermitte, Lhermitte, Lhermitte. The papers brought out special editions with photos and interviews and plans and details. A fresh load of horror! Was there no end to it? people wondered in desperation. No, there is no end to it. That's why we must pray for redemption.

Now the commotion has died down. She has in fact acquired formidable competition, although for now she need not fear demotion. She is still the tops, and I, the most hated woman in the country, the woman whose name is not and will not be forgotten, think of her. Not a day goes by without a thought of her. Call it an honorary salute.

Does she think of me?

If there is one thing there's no shortage of in a prison, it is time to reflect. Some days that is hell. *All* days.

By which I don't mean it's quiet.

God, my ears!

Rest is for the rest home.

But there too there will be the slamming of doors, and the wheeling of squeaking trolleys down the corridors. 'Soup, lovely soup!' If the old folk refuse to take their pills they are shouted at, or if they've wet their bed, or shat in it. Those old folk don't make much noise anymore. Their lungs are full of water. Blub blub. And if they do threaten to kick up a fuss, they get a bag over their head. Not a plastic bag, because then they will die and the rest home won't earn anymore from them. But you can pull a pillowslip over their heads, or a laundry bag. It's the same with parrots. They think it's night.

I always wanted a parrot. A green one that in the mornings would say to me: 'Hi, Odette. Sleep well, Odette? Fancy a cup of coffee, Odette?'

'Oh no,' said my mother, 'no parrot in my house!' A dog was OK. After lots of moaning and pleading. She chose the name: Fifi. And she decided which rooms the dog could go into, and from which rooms she was banned. And when Fifi died, she said: 'That's that. My house isn't a zoo. No zoology.'

It was *her* house. She had saved for it, together with my late father, God rest his soul. He was goodness itself, says everyone who knew him, with a heart of gold. And how different everything would have been if he had been granted more time on earth.

If I ever have a house of my own, a house I can furnish as I like, and where I can do what I like, and where no one comes and bosses me about or checks up on me, a house that is really my own, I'll buy a parrot. And I'll call him Coco. Coco Chanel.

I mustn't laugh, I mustn't laugh, I mustn't laugh.

Next thing it'll be in every paper: 'She has no remorse. She's laughing!'

And my poor Mummy, who at the end of her life was in a rest home and was too weak to visit me. *Ma pauvre petite maman chérie!* I would have so liked to look after you, as you looked after me. You never abandoned me, however difficult it was for you. I didn't want to abandon you either, but I couldn't visit you, I wasn't allowed to. Even for your funeral they wouldn't let me out. That was so awful, Mummy, not being able to say goodbye to you. I have known lots of black days here, but that day was jet black. What misery! Dear Mummy, what terrible things have happened to us? One catastrophe after the other. Who could have imagined it? Do you remember how happy we were, you and I? Sometimes it was difficult. You were having a difficult time, I was having a difficult time, we both suffered with our nerves, and we missed Daddy—oh, how we missed him!—but we had lovely moments too. And they won't come back. That is so cruel, Mummy. I'd so love to be little again, your little one. But now I have little ones of my own, three little ones, who are not so little anymore. How fast it goes!

Do you remember our delight when my first child was born? How full of hope we were, you and I. You didn't even have headaches anymore, 'I'm cured,' you said. 'That little mite is my medicine.'

I would so much have liked to make your nerves stronger, Mummy. I prayed and prayed. There was no more I could do.

They throw people into prison without thinking that they have a mother whom they have to look after. It's not easy being a good daughter when you're in prison, or a good mother. You have to fight, every day.

I fight. I have gone on fighting, like a lioness.

Sometimes I thought she was dead. She sat deathly still staring ahead of her. When I shook her gently, she said '*Je souffre*. I'm suffering.'

And I said: 'I'm here, Mummy, I'm your little one, your baby. I was in your tummy. If I could, I'd crawl back inside. Then we'd be together forever.'

I said: 'Shall I put a flannel on your forehead? Shall I get you a glass of milk? Shall I turn out the light, turn on the light, lower the blinds, raise the blinds?'

I'm suffering now too, Mummy, I've suffered so much. I didn't know a person could suffer so much, but still our suffering is nothing in comparison to the suffering of Jesus, Son of the Almighty, who is called Jehovah. Amen.

I remember everything, Mummy.

Every week our house was cleaned from top to bottom, even when there was no dirt, even when my mother was depressed. Turning the place inside out, my mother called it. 'We'll turn the place inside out. On Saturday mornings after breakfast she and I tied cloths over our hair. They weren't cloths, but worn-out scarves. Or ones that my mother considered worn-out. Ones she could not be seen in the street with without looking ridiculous. I could still manage it, she said, because I was young, and young people were less harshly judged, but that didn't last forever. Nothing lasted forever, certainly not youth. 'Have no illusions!'

She pulled the scarf off my head, braided my hair, rolled the braid up and fastened it with a hairpin. Now the scarf could go on top. And when was I going to cut all that hair off? It served no purpose, did it, all that hair? Was I planning to sell it? Had I let myself be talked into believing I could sell it? 'My daughter doesn't sell herself, understood?'

'Yes, Mummy. Of course, Mummy.'

'I wouldn't want…'

'I know, Mummy.'

Those words were sufficient to focus our minds on what bound us together forever: my dear Dad, who had loved us both deeply and we him. We lived in his house, and that's why we had to look after it. Mummy and Daddy had had the house built to be happy in with their daughter Odette, for whom they had had to wait a long time, almost fifteen years, which had made the joy at my birth all the more delirious. Unfortunately their happiness came to an abrupt end. Sweet songs don't last long.

Mummy and I put on rubber gloves and plastic aprons, armed ourselves with vacuum cleaner, buckets, mops and cleaning products, and went upstairs. In the bathroom Mummy filled the buckets with hot water. She added a dash of Mr Proper—with lemon!—and soaked the mop in it. 'Vacuuming isn't enough,' she said. 'People think they can solve everything with a hoover, but that's not true.' Meanwhile I turned on the vacuum cleaner and went to work. God help me if I left any dust! There must be no fluff on the mop later. Every bit of fluff was one too many, one that should have wound up in the vacuum cleaner.

'Is there still plenty of suction, Odette? Don't we need a new bag?'

'There's suction, Mummy.'

Three and a half hours later we pulled the front door open to scrub the threshold and the step. And then we scrubbed the threshold of the back door.

Every other week we cleaned the windows and needed an extra hour. But even then we didn't take a break. There was time for a break when we'd finished. And there was time for a bath too then, and for clean clothes. Exhausted, Mummy slumped into her chair, turned on the television and stared into space. Not a drop of energy was left. When I took her a cup of coffee, she sometimes did not have the strength to raise the cup to her lips. And if the TV guide slipped off her lap, she had to call me to pick it up for her.

She could not breathe in a house where there was dirt. Or where she thought there was dirt. But it took a lot out of her, too much. It wrecked her health.

'Odette is very good at cleaning,' M would say about me to his mates, in that special tone of his. Only a trained ear could hear the danger. Anyone who didn't know him didn't smell a rat. They called him friendly. Charming. In the mountains dogs start howling long before a human ear has picked up the first rumble of an avalanche. I was a dog like that. M had turned me into a dog. Not a St Bernard or an Alsatian like my faithful Brutus and Nero, but a Jack Russell, like Fifi: small but brave, and especially tireless. The way I worked for that man! Worked my fingers to the bone. And it was never enough.

'Odette, show us how well you can clean.' He kicked the waste bin over. 'Sorry. Accident.' Or he would pour milk on the ground, step into the puddle and leave a trail of milk all over the house.

'Thank you, M.' And then I mustn't forget to pull my mouth into a smile.

'Odette wasn't made to sit on her arse,' he said.

And why was that, M?

He himself had never had a mop in his hands. No one in that family had ever held a mop. His father hadn't, his mother hadn't, his brothers hadn't, his sister hadn't, and M definitely hadn't. He was even too lazy to wash himself. His parents had been in the Congo, at the very end, just before they chucked out all the whites. But they had been there long enough to learn how you could get others to do the dirty work for very little money. You had to pick young people and have them live in. That cost virtually nothing. At table they ate together with the whole gang. Now and then you stuck some pocket money in their hands and voilà, the housework was done for a song.

You could fuck them too. Those black women liked nothing better. 'Come here!' you had to say to them. You pointed to them and said: 'Come here.' And they would come. Those Congolese women fucked like we breathe. They could go on calmly working while they were being fucked. When nine months later a child rolled out of them they still went on working. They picked the child up, licked it clean, tied it onto their back, bent over their plot again and went on hoeing. Or they submerged their mop in a bucket, rinsed it, wrung it out thoroughly and went back to work. And a baby was never murdered by its mother. Never! White women could take a leaf out of their book.

It was there that M saw how cheap people are, and how easily new ones can be made.

He called me his '*pute*', or whore. It was meant as a term of affection. Or perhaps even a compliment. But I was less than his *pute*. I was a prostitute he didn't have to pay. His free *pute*.

His brothers should have stood up for themselves. They let themselves be treated as his servants, unpaid servants. They had to carry his satchel. He stuffed it full of comic strip books, but that was no problem, as he had porters. Those lads were no good for anything else, he said. 'Why do you think they've become postmen? They should be grateful to me, I trained them.'

Hahaha.

When his father told him to do the weeding, he called in his brothers. In life the art was to delegate, and to fool the naïve souls who wanted to be fooled.

He rented out the comic books at school at one franc a day. And from the proceeds he bought sweets, which he did not share with anyone.

He never shared anything with anyone. Ever.

His brothers should have demanded their fair share. They should have thrown his satchel on the ground. Carry your own rubbish!

The comic books were theirs too, but he acted as if they were his.

'The eldest son is the only one who counts. He is conceived with strong seed. The best of the father *and* the mother goes to him. His brothers and sisters have to make do with the remnants. In the Middle Ages the eldest son inherited *everything*: the estate, the house, and the serfs. Those who came after him had to go into a monastery, or on a crusade. Or they had to contrive to marry a rich daughter. One with a dowry.'

Yes, M. Of course, M.

'I'm the crown prince. Do you realise that?'

He didn't seem to realise that I was also the eldest. I was the eldest *and* the youngest. But I was a daughter, of course, an only daughter. *Une fille unique.*

'There are masters and there are servants, leaders and followers.' And he said he hadn't chosen to be a leader. A leader sacrifices himself. Day and night he works for the followers, even if the followers are too stupid to realise. In exchange the leader is entitled to respect. For example his satchel is carried for him. The tastiest food is for him, and the most fertile women. Where did I get the nerve to thrust a mop in his hands? What was the next step? An apron? Rubber gloves? He wasn't going to be turned into a girl. He wasn't the boy.

I was the boy. The *boyesse*.

A *boyesse* whom you could put through her paces at the fair.

They could exhibit Geneviève Lhermitte at the fair too. Five in a row. What mother could contend with her?

Suppose M's mother had done it. She needn't have killed all five. She could have stopped after M. She could have spared the future postmen, so that they could start delivering letters. Couldn't she have killed a single one? Was that asking too much?

She did not care about her children. Certainly not about M. Some women have children, but that doesn't make them mothers. M's mother could have had a hundred children, and she still wouldn't have become a mother. Never a good word for M, never. Nor for the others, but definitely not for M. He'd taken her youth, she said. It was his fault that she had been denied the carefree enjoyment of her young years, her best years. As if he had asked her to get pregnant! The other four she could manipulate. Not him. Bitching from morning till night. She wasn't embarrassed about me. A normal woman wants to make a good impression on a new daughter-in-law, but she...

She certainly liked being pregnant. Why else would she have child after child, without concerning herself about them? Children didn't interest her. And their father didn't interest her either. Sex interested her, yes, but she could have taken precautions.

With each child the father wondered if he was the father. And then they're surprised when M...

She liked them young too, didn't she? In the Congo she was caught with one of her pupils, by her own husband. The boy was under age. If it had happened here, she would never have been allowed to teach again. But as it was the Congo, everything was possible. Those whites protected each other. If ever there was networking, it was there.

The father wasn't any better. Now he says that she started it, but who believes that? To begin with he was out there alone. M was safely in Mummy's tummy. They both thought it better if M made his entrance in Belgium. Cooey, here I am.

What does a man alone do in the Congo? He says he set up a chess club. Everywhere he went he set up chess clubs. If they'd sent him to the moon, he would have set up a chess club there. But no one plays chess twenty-four hours a day.

And supposing that she started it, even then he didn't have to follow her example. Have I ever followed M's example?

After all those years he still couldn't stop talking about his African princesses, not even to me. What father-in-law does that? And you had to say 'kuyuku' to them. Then they would come. And you could fondle their breasts. They were as hard as wood. He maintained.

As if those things interested me.

I had said to M that we should invite his father over. Gilles should get to know his grandfather. I felt. I also knew that my father-in-law would not be organising any Santa Claus parties for his grandchildren, or taking them to the Efteling and Walibi, but there had to be someone to whom Gilles could say 'Granddad'. The first thing he announced when he came in was that he didn't wish to be called 'Granddad', or 'Pappy' or 'Pop'. The grandchildren should call him by his first name. Why? No explanation. And then he started talking about the mulatto women he had had. And about their ebony breasts.

M liked white women. The whiter the better. That's why he went to Eastern Europe so often. To the Caucasus, where the white race has its roots. The Caucasian race. M did not want any black women. Or women with hard breasts. What normal man wants a woman with hard breasts?

All those men who went to the Congo had only a single aim. But they were never punished. No, no. They were heroes.

When M's mother's nerves got bad, she started hitting out. She hit people straight in the face. M was also hit by her. M! He didn't hit back, ever. 'I ignored it,' he said. 'Surely you don't think she's ever hurt me?'

But she *could* have hurt him. The woman could floor anyone. She had a black belt. Fortunately I did not know that the first time I saw her. I wouldn't have dared to shake hands with her! She started in the Congo. There was a judo club there. It turned out that she had talent. My father also tried, but couldn't do it. She could. Mama M had not been idle in the Congo. She used her time as a colonial well.

If only they had stayed in the Congo! M could have been Mr Big there, with ten women on each finger.

She gave judo lessons at home. Special mats were put down, said M, but the whole house shook when yet another person was thrown to the floor. Wham!

'And why didn't you learn judo?' I asked him.

'I don't need it,' he replied.

The woman was always out and about, and her husband too. Evening after evening the children were left alone. He went to play chess and she went to judo class. They had no time to read their children a story and they had no time to go to the parents' evenings, but for the chess club and the judo club they had all the time in the world. And then they're amazed when things turn out badly. They had nothing to give their children, nothing at all.

The two of them lived as if they had no children. She didn't have to murder her children. Why would she have murdered them?

Is it possible that murderess-mothers kill their children because they love them? Love them too much? If that is true, then maybe it's too dangerous to love your children a whole lot, then it's better... No, you can never love your children enough. Those mothers don't love their children. They think they love them, but it's not love, it's... I don't know what it is, but it isn't love, it isn't love, it isn't love.

M could sometimes respond so feebly when I was loving with him. As if he didn't understand. Actually he didn't respond at all. He wasn't angry and he wasn't happy. He was nothing.

When we were first together I used to buy him presents, but he did not seem to know what to do with them. I had to unwrap them myself. Otherwise they would have stayed where I put them down, wrapped and with the ribbon round them. My first present to him was a deodorant, because well, I felt his personal hygiene could do with improvement. 'Why are you giving me that?' he said. I thought I had insulted him. I apologised and said that I certainly didn't want to suggest that he didn't smell nice. He smelled nice, but he didn't wash enough and went round for too long in the same clothes. Men paid less attention to that. Because in addition he did physical work, he sweated and so I thought that deodorant might help, although there was nothing wrong with his sweat as such. The smell of sweat could even be a turn-on sometimes. In the middle of my explanation he turned round and left. I stood there with my deodorant. I didn't know what to do with it. It was a deodorant for men. I wasn't going to use it. I put it on the draining board in the kitchen. A little later it had gone. He must have taken it, because I didn't touch it and there were no goblins in our house.

I bought a belt for him, a dark-blue one in supple leather and a nice copper-coloured buckle. Made in Italy. Again the same reaction: 'Why are you giving me that?' I thought he felt the buckle was too flashy, or that blue wasn't masculine enough. I'll give the belt to my cousin, I thought. He'll like it. That evening I saw him wearing the belt. 'Ah,' I said, 'you do like it after all.' He didn't react. 'The belt,' I said. No reaction. 'That blue suits you.' Still nothing. It was as if he didn't want to admit that I had given him the belt. He was pretending that he had always had it. He wore it for years. When he changed trousers, he pulled it out of one pair and passed it through the loops of the other. It was slightly too wide, and it was always a bit of a squeeze, but eventually he got very good at it. There were days when I was afraid that he would hit me with the belt, but that never happened. M didn't need a belt for that.

The last present I gave him was a tool box I had seen in Brico. I had actually gone to look for a barbecue on wheels. When I got there all the barbecues had gone, but they had a whole wall of tool boxes. They were piled up to the ceiling. That's just the thing for M, I thought. He had lots of tools, but they were a clutter of things he had collected over the years. He was always complaining because he was messing around with useless tools. Many of them he had stolen. If you haven't paid for it you've no right to complain. I think. But he complained anyway. In the store they assured me that my husband would be happy with it. It wasn't top quality, that was impossible at that price, but it was sturdy and could be used every day. I took the box home as pleased as Punch. I had had it wrapped in shiny paper. He couldn't miss it. I put the shiny package on the television. Two days later it was still there. 'Don't you want to know what's in it?' I asked. He didn't even answer.

He didn't trust those presents. He saw them as a trap. He was afraid I would take them from him again and throw them away. Or destroy them. Or that I would give them to someone else, as his father had done with the carpentry set that he had been given by his Granny and Granddad. In his first year at school M came home at Christmas with a brilliant report. He had got top marks in virtually everything. That isn't that difficult in your first year, but he managed it. His parents didn't say a word about it, either positive or negative, nothing. They scarcely looked at the report. But his Granny and Granddad wanted to reward him. They gave him a case with a hammer, a saw, a chisel and a file. M was so happy and proud! He never played with it. His parents gave it away to another child. That tool box from the DIY store was of course the most stupid possible present. When I finally took off the gift wrapping myself, his face froze. Just like a mask. A few days later his brother dropped by. I thought: I'll give him the box. He then told me about the case full of carpentry tools that his parents had given away. If his brother had not told me the sad story, I would never have known. M kept those things to himself. He was too proud to talk about them.

His brother didn't want the box. Finally I put it in the van with all the other tools. Nothing was ever said about it. But he did use it. From then on I always did it in that way. When I had bought something for him, I put it in his cupboard or in the place where he would use it, but I didn't make a present of it. The memories were too painful, for him. I went on buying stuff for him. When I saw something I thought he needed, I bought it. If I had the money. At the beginning it was easier, before he started checking my outgoings. I didn't have much leeway, because M couldn't stand me spending money frivolously. Not that I've ever done that. Mummy had taught me the value of money. She had been through the war, and Dad too.

More than once I thought: oh, if only I could have given you some love from the moment you were born!

Love didn't interest him. Sex did, but love didn't. Because he had never known it. He didn't know what it was. He couldn't recognise it, he couldn't give it, he couldn't receive it.

The worst thing was that he realised that. Sometimes.

There were moments when he realised. Then he knew very well why he was the person he was and what he was like.

I tried to straighten out what had grown crooked, but it was too late.

It was as if love could gain no hold on him. It slid off him.

At school we had had to read *Le petit prince*. I knew the book well, because I did an exam on it and later even gave a teaching-practice lesson on it. I loved it, especially the passage about the fox who asks the little prince to make him tame and explains to him how to do it, with superhuman patience. First the little prince must keep his distance and mustn't say anything, but gradually he is allowed to come a little closer each day. The fox needed time to get used to the prince.

I thought it would be the same with M. I had hoped to tame him step by step, the way the little prince tames the fox, with love and patience.

I thought: I'll prove to him that he can trust me, that I won't drop him. I shall prove that love exists, unconditional love, real love. I shall give him the love that he had to do without. And that love will cure him.

I really thought that.

I saw him as a man with a gaping hole where his heart should be. *Un homme avec un trou*. I wanted to fill that hole. I felt pain in his place. I felt pain because it didn't cause him pain. Or because he *thought* that it didn't cause him pain.

When I think of it, it still causes me pain.

In his first year, his parents sent him to school on the train. He wasn't yet six. They didn't take him to the station, no, no. He walked over a kilometre to the station by himself, took the train and got off at the next station. Then it was another quarter of an hour through the town to the school. At four o'clock he had to do the same journey, but in the opposite direction. And he had to make sure he got the right train. Only the slow train stopped in his village. He couldn't mistake it. But of course other trains stopped at the station near his school. How could a child make that distinction? At the beginning he couldn't yet read, could he? But God help him if he made a mistake.

The following year they sent his brother with him. Two little boys alone on the train. They could have been abducted! And that while there was a school in the village where they lived. But they didn't consider it good enough. His parents were both primary school teachers. They looked after other children at yet another school. They could have taken their sons with them to that school. But no. The father was at loggerheads with all his colleagues. He didn't trust them.

At first I refused to believe it. I thought M was pulling the wool over my eyes, but his father started talking about it. He thought it was perfectly normal. That's what happened in the Congo. There, children were sent to the spring to fetch water. Children were given responsibility from a very early age. A child of five carried his brother or sister, who couldn't yet walk, on his back. And a can of water on his head, or firewood. That strengthened their backbone, literally and figuratively.

The worst thing was that it was against the law. A child of five is not allowed to take the train unaccompanied. That's why it stopped after two years, because the railway authorities finally realised that that little chap and his brother were on the train alone every day.

It took them a long time to realise.

The father was particularly afraid that the children would be spoilt. Spoiling children—*that* was the great danger that must be avoided. Leaving children to their fate, that was OK. Neglecting them: fine. Spoiling yourself, there was nothing wrong with that. Stuffing yourself in front of the children with the sweets you had confiscated from them: great. Because sweets were bad for their teeth. But not for yours.

Had he seen that in the Congo too?

And of course M took after him. And I kept trying to give a different example. And hoped the children would follow my example.

Il faut partager.

You must share.

Try teaching that to a child when its own father keeps everything for himself.

The mother would have done better to murder M. She could have said it was an accident. Accidents happen all the time. Most accidents happen at home. Fatal accidents too, especially those. People are careful everywhere except in their own home. They think they are safe there. They let themselves go. Even M. let himself go at home sometimes. Sometimes.

There is no such thing as safety. Anywhere. She must have known that. Why else did she want to learn judo? A normal woman doesn't learn judo. Certainly not when she has five children. She stays at home and looks after her children. Period. Perhaps she takes cookery classes, or sewing lessons, or yoga. But judo? No.

She could have finished him off with a judo hold and afterwards she could have said that he had had a fall. She could have laid him at the bottom of the stairs, as if he had fallen down them. She always maintained that he was no good, that she had always known. She should have been consistent and taken responsibility. It would have been a trifle for her.

Lhermitte did not know judo. Neither did her rival. Those women began something without realising what they had begun. They were not prepared. And so they could not see it through. According to plan Lhermitte should have killed herself too. And her rival should have killed all her five children. But after the third child she faltered, like an engine that sputters because the fuel tank springs a leak. Caused by whom, by what? Don't ask questions, Odette. There's a leak, OK?

Sometimes things go your way, sometimes they go against you.

Man proposes, fate disposes.

A panic attack, writes one.

An epileptic fit, maintains the other.

I say: an epileptic fit caused by panic.

If I have learned one thing from M, it is not to give in to panic. He did not know what panic was. He didn't know what love was and he didn't know what panic was either. That sometimes makes life easy, you know, not knowing what feelings are. Feelings get in the way. Not always, but often. And of course M had feelings. He felt pain, rage and indignation. They are feelings too.

Perhaps panic is more of a reaction than a feeling, but that is no excuse. You must learn to control reactions too. When they arrested me in front of my children, when they led me away in handcuffs, when they took me away in a wailing police car... I didn't feel a moment's panic. I knew that panic wouldn't help me. On the contrary.

Cool head, cool head, cool head. Make the best of a bad job.

Now too. Definitely now.

Anyone who lets themselves be carried away by panic is giving up, said M. And humiliating themselves. He had seen that often enough in the girls he dragged into his van. They wet themselves. He found that embarrassing for them. Extremely embarrassing.

M never gave up. Not even when he had lost.

If you ask me he still hasn't given up.

If she had not had that panic-epileptic attack, she could have beaten Lhermitte: murdering five children and herself too.

Lhermitte wouldn't have liked that. No more gold medal for Geneviève Lhermitte!

Now her rival didn't have a chance. She collapsed like the twin towers in New York. She lay there like a sack of potatoes. The two children she had not yet murdered rushed to her aid. 'Mummy, Mummy what's wrong?' They wanted to help their Mummy, their dear Mummy. They rang for an ambulance. And they fetched the woman from next door. She came as soon as she could and also brought her little son with her. What chance did that woman have with all those people in her house?

M. would say that the plan was no good, but even he could not always foresee everything. If he had foreseen everything I wouldn't be in here now. And he wouldn't be in there. The two most hated inmates, each in their own prison. Mirror, mirror in the wall, who's the most hated one of all, him or me?

They've thrown Lhermitte in jail, but where has her rival been dumped: prison, hospital or madhouse?

In love, engaged, married. In love, engaged, prison. In love, engaged, madhouse. In love, engaged, hospital. They've probably put her in a madhouse. A madhouse specialising in epilepsy.

Whenever the moon is full and round in the sky, it crackles in their heads. They fall to the ground like lumps. White foaming saliva leaks from their mouths. They jerk like a bad actor faking orgasm. 'They can choke,' said my mother. 'Sometimes they swallow their own tongue and they choke.' She had once seen one, on the tram. She was on her way to the parents of my father, to whom she had just got engaged. 'Leave the tram!' ordered the conductor sternly, but no one wanted to miss the spectacle, and neither did my mother, a young bride-to-be. Imagine: a German officer in uniform whose trembling body is filling the aisle. The arms were flailing, the legs were stamping. Urine was streaming from him.

My mother had wanted to throw herself on the epileptic. She had kicked off her shoes and had slid to the edge of the seat. She placed her hands to the left and right of her thighs, ready to push off for the leap. Her body would calm his, like a blanket thrown on the flames. The realisation that she would become part of the spectacle stopped her at the last moment.

Nothing would have stopped me.

When the conductor had finally thrown the passengers off his tram, my mother realised that urine had leaked from her too. Not as much as from the German officer, but enough to feel it. Was there a stain on her dress? On her coat? Oh, the shame, the shame! And now there was also a ladder in her new stockings. What on earth was happening? She had bought the stockings especially for the visit to her future parents-in-law, although it was wartime. Stockings cost a fortune, but her mama had said: 'If you're serious about that man, you must wear stockings.'

The other stranded passengers had carried her along with them to a bar. She had tried in vain to drink the Dutch gin a fellow passenger had offered her. Her teeth were chattering against the rim of the glass. Someone said that she must eat, but she couldn't swallow a thing. The ambulance siren drove them all back out into the street. They saw the epileptic being taken away on a stretcher and disappearing into the belly of the ambulance. The tram continued on its way, but my mother could not bring herself to get on. She felt exhausted and soiled as if she had had sex with the pissing, foaming man in the aisle in full view of all the passengers. She would have liked nothing better than to break off the engagement.

At home she took off her clothes and threw them

away, not into the laundry basket, but into the rubbish bin. War or no war, she did not want to wear them anymore, she could not wear them any more.

First she soaked in the bath, and then she scrubbed herself clean at the washbasin. But the gagging man still clung to her. He never disappeared from her head or from her body.

'That day evil was planted in my womb,' she often said.

Because she and my father were respectable people. *Des gens convenables*. And so were their parents. I couldn't have got it from them.

If I was fathered by that sick ss officer on that Sunday afternoon, it was a pregnancy of over sixteen years. Long enough for a Devil's child.

But I was not fathered in that tram.

Sometimes they turn into wolves.

That isn't true.

M could turn into a wolf, a wolf that stands on its hind legs so that everyone can see its penis. His wolf's penis. It was a test. He wanted to see whether I would get into a panic. I forced myself to stay calm. I folded my hands and prayed. In my mind I folded my hands. If I had really done it, he would have torn me to pieces with his wolf's teeth, his wolf's claws.

Wolves are less dangerous than people think. They attack when they have no other choice. Actually they are frightened of people.

Don't force me, M often said.

I didn't force him. I tried not to force him.

Sometimes I forced him without realising, or I realised too late. With that story of my mother's about the epileptic, for example. I thought it would amuse him, and it did seem to amuse him. I could have sworn that he giggled when I told him how my mother, with wet knickers, was ready to jump on the poor man in the midst of a full tram. It made me reckless. I made up details to extend my moment of triumph, and laid it on thick. Pathetic, I know, and unforgivable. I heard myself rattling on, though I knew perfectly well that people rattling on drove M nuts. He let me tell the story. He didn't interrupt me. And then suddenly there was his hand over my mouth and four grim words: my brother has epilepsy.

Which brother? I didn't dare ask. He had so many.

'Forgive me,' I said. 'Please tell me you forgive me.'

'There's no point,' he said. 'I can forgive you and you'll do it again tomorrow.'

He didn't hit me that time. I wasn't even worth the effort.

2

The murderess-mother, the mother-murderess lies on the ground in the living room of her house. Sunlight streams in through the tall windows, but that isn't much good to her right now. She thrashes about like a fish that has just been landed. Her mouth goes gulp, gulp. In her fall she has pulled the cloth off the table. It is now lying half on top, half underneath her. Fortunately there was no vase on the table, fortunately there was no water in the vase, fortunately there were no flowers in the vase, fortunately the cloth, well, the cloth is cotton, and can go straight in the washing machine. Thirty degrees, no prewash necessary.

The woman likes to keep her house neat and tidy. In the light of events everyone would regard shards and broken-off flowers as a negligible detail. Not her. Nothing is a detail for her. Everything must be in perfect order. Everything must be in perfect order. Everything must...

Shush, darling, shush.

She has hit her shoulder on a chest of drawers. In the hospital the doctor will notice and record the bruise, but won't draw any conclusions. The doctor has an open mind. Prejudgements are alien to him, as is rushed work. He strives for scientific rigour and objectivity. Her husband does too, but her husband is not home. He is Dutch, an engineer with a demanding job. For now no one thinks it necessary to inform him of the drama unfolding in his house. For now it isn't a drama for anyone. An epileptic fit is not a drama. On the other side of the ceiling are the cots with the bodies of the three youngest children, but for now the mother is the only one who knows that. And probably she doesn't know herself anymore. A lightning bolt has struck her brain. It has yanked the glasses off her nose and thrown them obliquely onto her face. It sends electric shocks through her nerves. The neighbour who has been summoned to help does not dare touch her, for fear of also getting a shock, and she also keeps her little son away from the epileptic. From a safe distance she makes soothing noises, though she doubts their effect. She tells the children that everything will be all right. There's no reason to panic. She says it without believing it herself.

'Listen, there's the ambulance already. It will look after your mummy.'

Knock, knock, who's there?

She smiles a reassuring smile, although she feels anything but reassured. She knows that she's going to have a sleepless night and that her son will have nightmares again later. If this goes on, she thinks, they will have to move. For her neighbour's children it is different. They've become used to their mother's attacks by now.

The ambulance crew come into the house. They know the woman and they know the family. It's not the first time that they've screeched to a halt in the drive to give first aid. 'Where are the three little ones?' one of them wants to know, while the other tends to the mother. 'Upstairs,' says the eldest son. 'Mummy has given them a bath.' The paramedic looks at the neighbour, who interprets his look as a request, which it is. She goes upstairs. 'They're in their beds,' she says when she comes back downstairs. 'They're sleeping like logs.'

Dull-witted neighbour. Who can't tell the difference between a dead child and a sleeping child? And dull-witted ambulance men, because why would the mother put the tiny tots back in bed after their morning bath? At night it's bath then bed, and in the morning it's exactly the other way round.

You have to test the temperature with your elbow. Before you dip the baby in the water, you must check with your elbow that the water is not too hot, or too cold. Too cold is less bad than too hot. Children can stand cold better than heat. In the winter it was always a struggle with Gilles to get him to put his coat on. And a hat he would always pull off. So I asked M for money to buy Gilles a hat with flaps for the ears and cords you can tie. Gilles was so angry. He just kept tugging at that hat. The harder he tugged at the cords the tighter the knot became. 'He has my stubbornness, said M, 'but not my brains.'—'Yes, darling,' I said. 'That's true.' And I gave him a butterfly kiss: brushing his lips with mine.

Sometimes I think: if I could begin anew, I'd do everything just the same. You can't choose in life. You can't say: I want the main course, but not the aperitif, or the dessert, or the liqueur. You can't say: I want my children but not him. You have to go via him to have the children. And those children are wonderful. Even Lhermitte would not have killed them.

But that neighbour, then, really thought that those children were sleeping peacefully in their beds. And the paramedics believed her. Why shouldn't they? They took the mother to the hospital and left the neighbour in a house with three dead bodies in it.

They will probably all be wondering: 'Couldn't we have saved the children? Isn't it partly our fault?

How often that has been said about me: she could have saved them. Throw her in prison, because she could have saved them. She must never be released, because she could have saved them. She did nothing to save them, though she could have saved them. She deserves the death penalty, because she could have saved them.

Again and again, like a record stuck in a groove.

I've been in prison for sixteen years because I didn't save them although I could have saved them. So they say. They weren't there, but they know for sure that I could have saved those girls.

If it were all so simple.

Perhaps the paramedics and the neighbour could have saved the tiny tots, but they're not in prison. They are getting psychological help to deal with the trauma.

The father did not save his children either. He was in a meeting while his wife was suffocating his children. With laughing gas, they say. How did she get hold of laughing gas? Can anyone tell me how she got hold of that laughing gas? Who sold it to her? Shouldn't the seller have asked what she planned to do with it? Can anyone in this country who wants to murder someone just buy laughing gas? And where do you buy it?

I hope that neighbour will feel guilty for the rest of her life. And the paramedics too, who were too stupid to go and check on the children for themselves. Let it gnaw at them, eat them up, like maggots eating a corpse.

It would have been too late to save them, wrote the papers.

How can they be so sure? Why is it too late in one case and not in the other?

Their brother found them: a boy of eleven who had to find his dead brothers and sisters. Even for a gifted child that is appalling.

Gilles was eleven when we were arrested, right in front of him. That's an age at which they're very aware of everything. It leaves its mark.

I don't know if the three murdered children were in the same room. That wasn't in any newspaper.

Journalists can't know everything. They do their best, but they can't perform magic. Sometimes they have to dig and dig in order to find answers.

I always cooperated. When someone asked me a question I answered, even if I didn't know the answer.

It's better to give some kind of answer than none.

That's what they said at school when you had to take an exam.

If you say nothing, you make a stupid impression, or a dull one. Here in prison too I answer all questions. It's a matter of politeness.

The children were highly gifted. And the mother was ill. There was epilepsy and another disease the doctors can't really say much about. My Mummy and I experienced that. My Mummy was always tired, just like that woman. When my mother had cleaned the house, she couldn't get out of her chair for the rest of the week. But she didn't kill me. I never thought for a second: now she's going to murder me. What child thinks that of its mother? No one expects something like that.

That mother was close to despair. She didn't know which way to turn. She thought: I'm going to die soon and there'll be no one to look after my gifted children. She couldn't send them to school. She could, but her children were bored out of their skulls. So she kept them at home and taught them herself. What was to happen to her children when she was no longer there?

And so they've always got an explanation.

There can never be any pity for women who murder their children. However sick they are. *They* are sick, not their children.

What are they to do next? Can she see her children? What does she say to them, or to her husband? And what does he say to her? Does he still live in that house? Does he sleep in the bed he slept in with her? Where their children were conceived? And where does she sleep?

The papers don't write anything about that. They can't stop writing about me, but not another word about her. As if it never happened. Let's forget it. Hush it up. They must have paid off the journalists.

An invaluable piece of advice, sir: go back to Holland. Take the remaining children with you and leave your wife in Belgium. Forget her. She doesn't exist, she never existed. And no pity, especially not that. There are no excuses for what she did. Epilepsy! Does she really think that other people don't have problems?

According to Anouk many women in here pretend to have epileptic fits. They lie squirming on the floor of their cells. Or they bang their heads against the wall, supposedly because they're hearing voices. Some women will go to any lengths to get attention.

'We don't let anyone die,' says Anouk. 'If someone

really needs nursing, they get it. But women who play-act we ignore. Or we give them a laxative.'

They've never given me a laxative.

I'm going the right way, says Anouk. The way that leads to the exit. I can smell the outside air. When I breathe in deeply, I can smell it.

A day seldom goes by here when you don't hear an ambulance. Beepobeepobeepo. Perhaps they are police cars. I never used to pay attention to whether there is a difference between the siren of an ambulance and that of a police car. And I paid no attention to the murderess-mothers either. I didn't read any papers. When I had to take the children to the doctor's, I leafed through the magazines in the waiting room, that was all. I didn't follow the news. Neither did M. We had no time.

Sister Virginie says that the nuns in the convent watch the news every day at one o'clock and at seven, and that I can watch with them. 'We're not unworldly,' she says. 'How could we pray for the world if we didn't know the world?' How could they have prayed for me if they hadn't followed the stream of reports about me? And then she opens her prayer book and shows the photo of me in her missal. My photo in a prayer book!

I will realise, she says, that most people have a completely wrong idea of life in a convent.

Most people have a completely wrong idea of life in a prison too.

That's true, she says. And that she will miss her visits to the prison once I am living with them. And no, she doesn't intend to choose another prisoner to take pity on. God sent her to me.

She talks as if it is all sewn up: my release, my move to the convent, my welcome by the sisters. She has even already made my bed up. And no, it is not as narrow as the one I have to sleep in here. That is more of a camp bed than a conventional bed.

'Hope is poison,' I say.

'Despair is poison,' she corrects me.

'What is the first thing you want to do when they let you out?' Or: 'What would you do now, at this moment, if you were free?'

Most women answer: go shopping. If they answer. Or: have a bath with lots of bath foam or oil. Because here we can only shower. And a new towel every day, because here we have to dry ourselves for a week with the same one. And then they start talking about brands and smells and colours, and about a bath in the shape of a heart or a shell or a square bath, or a bath with a jacuzzi, and that goes on until you have the feeling you've had a bath. No kidding.

Or they say: lying in bed all day with my man. With a man, it doesn't matter who. Renting a gigolo, spreading jam on my nipples and all over my sex and making him lick it up. Not jam but honey, or chocolate paste.

And then there's always one who pretends she has heard 'all over my legs'. 'What? Jam all over your legs?'

'Sex!'

And she says they can start practising, as you don't need a man for that.

Don't hear that smut. Don't think of the hours in bed with M and a girlfriend of his. He called her Sasha, because in the skating rink she wore a white fur hat, and a fur muff. Real chinchilla. She claimed. Stolen from her godmother's wardrobe. Sometimes she put the hat on in bed. And she stroked my back with the muff. So soft! And M was jealous because I sucked her nipples, but we couldn't both suck his penis, could we? I had to leave *his* nipples alone. He couldn't stand me touching them, so I sucked her nipples. Or bit them gently. What else was I supposed to do? Stare at the ceiling?

And later, while the two of them were at it, I got out of bed and danced bare-arsed with the muff as my only item of clothing. I fluttered through the room, I sang and leapt about, and those two stopped to look at me. I swear it's true! They preferred looking at me to going on fucking, I was so beautiful. Beautiful and elegant and attractive, and strong, really strong.

He'll get up and come to me, I thought. He'll want to stick his prick in me. And he got up. His prick was gleaming with the moisture from her cunt. He bore down on me like a knight with his lance, and she got out of bed too, they both wanted to be with me. I went on dancing and dancing, while they grabbed me and kissed me and licked me. I, Odette, was their queen. Their mighty queen, their Salome.

I know what some women here do with each other, but I don't join in, ever. Not even if I want to terribly. It would be a trap. The next day it would be all over the papers. I would be called the instigator, the violator. The things I've experienced here! Indescribable. And the worst ones are those who come on friendly.

This is my greatest fear: that Sister Virginie is setting a trap for me. That she is making me believe that I can go and live in the convent, only to pull out at the last moment and make fun of me. You fell for it! Then she tears the crucifix from her neck, and spits on it. Who says that she's really a nun? What if the devil has sent her?

'You don't have to trust me, my child. Trust in God.'

But perhaps I'm the gullible sod.

She mustn't think that I'm going to pray with her every day in that convent. Or that I'm always going to watch the news with them. And she definitely mustn't think... but no, they're too old for that, and too chaste.

You never know these things of course.

'In that area a mother doesn't know her own daughter.' My mother said.

But later she said: 'I always knew.'

And she said: 'Rotten to the core.'

She had said to me about her sex life: 'I always let your father have his way. If he wanted sex while I was having my period, we had sex while I was having my period. If he wanted to lick me while I was having my period, I let him lick me while I was having my period. That's the best thing a woman can do. If she wants to keep her man, if she's serious about him.'

Of course it's the best thing.

My father thought that women were infertile during menstruation, said my mother. That's how it began. And when he knew better, he went on doing it.

Each to his own.

My mother lost far more blood than I did. And for longer, for seven or eight days at a time. I always knew when she had her period, because the sheets were dirty. 'My blood's too thin,' she said. 'It gushes out.'

We left the sheets as they were until after her menstruation. There was no point in putting clean sheets on since the next morning they were dirty again.

My father had damaged something inside. She didn't want to admit it, but it was true. He was a saint for her. He was a man. They could do whatever they liked. They wrote the rules themselves.

I never want a man again.

Never. Again.

'They all want the same thing, Odette. There's not one you can rely on. Except for the gays, but they're not men.'

And I wanted it too. I wanted it too.

I felt it in my stomach, in my cunt, in my throat.

Oh yes. Now. Please, please, please. Don't stop. There, yes. More. And hoping you won't have to beg. That he won't stop before it comes. And that he won't notice how badly I want it.

But I don't want it any more now. I don't want to want it anymore.

'You must pray, my child.'

'Yes, sister. I shall pray.

I pray.

Even after I'm released I shall pray. I shall pray in the chapel, and I shall pray in my room, and in the kitchen and the dining room and in the garden. I shall pray the whole time, everywhere. I shall even pray in the bathroom. Lead me not into temptation, lead me not into temptation. And thank you for this chance, and forgive me, forgive me. I shall be like the Hare Krishnas we sometimes saw in Charleroi, Hooray Krishnas, M called them, but without a tambourine or pink and ochre robes, and I won't shave my head either, and of course I won't sing Hare Krishna but Hail Mary full of Grace the Lord be with you the Lord be with you the Lord be with you. They should lock those maniacs up, said M. Christ, a person could no longer do his shopping at his leisure in his own town. Yes, M, of course, M, it's a disgrace, M. I would have liked to walk with them, think of nothing, Hare Krishna, Hare Krishna, pray for us poor sinners and blessed is Jesus, the fruit of your womb, *le fruit de vos entrailles, priez pour nous, pauvres pécheurs*, poor sinners, *maintenant et à l'heure de notre mort*, pray for us poor sinners now and in the hour of our death our death our death.

And when I have prayed enough, perhaps I'll go to the hairdresser, a real hairdresser who takes the time to massage my scalp, and treats my hair with lotions, and asks if I'd like a coffee and then brings me a cup with a biscuit, or a praline. A hairdresser who calls me 'madam'. 'What would madam like?' 'Did madam have a particular style in mind?' 'May we recommend madam our new shampoo?' 'Is madam considering colouring her hair?'

Madam considers whether she is considering it.

Even the nuns don't pray twenty-four hours a day.

Do they go to the hairdresser? Do they cut each other's hair? Or their own hair?

Sister Virginie's hair looks as if she cuts it herself. Fortunately she doesn't shave it, and so she won't ask me to shave my hair off.

Those poor women after the war... And they just went with the Germans so they could eat. What were they supposed to do? Let themselves starve like the Jews in the camps?

A person's first duty is to survive.

Thanks be to God that they did not shave my hair off here in prison. If He wishes I will cover it with a cloth. With a scarf. Like Audrey Hepburn and Cathérine Deneuve, or Jackie Kennedy. Or like my mother when she came back from the hairdresser. And cleaned the house, in her weekly battle against dirt, which was mine too. My battle, I mean. And my dirt, I assume.

Please let me go to the hairdresser, God. And perhaps

to a beauty salon too. I have never set foot in a beauty salon. They say you feel reborn. The pores of your face are opened up with steam for deep cleansing. All the dirt in your body evaporates. You feel reborn, just as our house was reborn every Saturday.

Me in a beauty salon. *Un institut de beauté.*

I'll give it a try.

If I could choose, if someone were to say: go ahead and choose, do what you like—I'd go to the hairdresser at the seaside. First a beauty salon, then a hairdresser, and then shopping. Not necessarily to buy anything but simply to see what is in the shop windows. *Lèche-vitrines.* And perhaps going in somewhere and buying something after all, for me or the children. And eating mussels washed down with a glass of wine. All in one day. In Knokke. Or Le Coq. Or Ostend. But not in Blankenberge. And definitely not in Middelkerke.

My parents-in-law used to have a chalet in Middelkerke. On a campsite. They called it a 'chalet' but it was no more than a glorified caravan, a shed. Of course that mustn't be said and stupid Odette could not keep her big mouth shut, and went rattling on about Knokke this and Knokke that, and how sweet the little shop was where my mother bought her gloves every year. It was such a funny sight, all those gloved hands on pedestals in the window. Leather gloves, yes yes, calf, that was the supplest.

Forget it, Odette. It was stupid of you, you got your punishment, your well-deserved punishment. You learned to hold your tongue, and you owe him a debt of gratitude for that, down to the present. How would you have kept afloat here if you hadn't learnt to hold your tongue? Speaking is silver, silence is golden. He can't do any more to you. Not even when you're released. Then you'll be able to go to Knokke as often as you want. And he won't. He can't even go to Blankenberge or to Middelkerke. He can only go from one prison to another, from one courtroom to another, till he drops dead.

Idiot, who thought he could escape.

I'll escape, he won't. When I leave this prison, I will do it surrounded by police officers, lawyers, judges, bailiffs, warders, magistrates, and a document in my hand with signatures and stamps and seals, perhaps even that of the king, who trembles and shivers, and who held the country together so bravely when M and I had turned it on its head. So that they can't shut me up again, ever. And then I'll go to the seaside. One fine day I'll go to the seaside. Nothing and no one will stop me. And I'll go and eat a *dame blanche* in the Titanic. If it still exists.

Much will have changed. I must be prepared for that, says Anouk. It will be a shock. And I won't be able to return to prison if I want to.

Does she really think I shall want to do that?

The Titanic was called the Titanic because the owner's grandmother had gone down with the ship. She had a rich, sickly friend, who had paid for both their passages. The friend wanted company. A woman alone day and night on a boat like that gives men ideas, even if she is sickly. 'Now, be careful,' said my mother, 'some women are out for that. They like nothing better.' My mother was not that kind of woman. Neither was I.

The ice creams in the Titanic were served in boat-shaped dishes and named after ships. You could get a catamaran, or a barge, a sloop, a yacht, a rowing boat, a tanker, a tug, a schooner, a galleon and naturally also a titanic. That was the most expensive, and the most delicious. If my mother was in a good mood, she would order two titanics. And a glass of elixir for herself. I was too young for that. Later, she said, when I was married. Then I would also have to have my hair cut and have a perm. And I would sip elixir, the only strong drink a respectable woman could afford to drink in public without jeopardising her reputation.

The walls of the ice-cream parlour were decorated with photos of the Titanic and the drowned grandmother. You saw passengers cheerfully embarking and waving large white handkerchiefs at the people on the quayside and at the brass band, which was still playing. A circle had been drawn in black ink around the face of one of the waving figures. 'Emilie?' someone had written beside it. The last photo was of a lifeboat with about ten people in it. They were all that was left of that laughing, waving crowd.

The friend had neither a husband nor children, but the grandmother did. Her sons were three, five and eight years old at the time. Their portraits were also hanging there, as children on their Mummy's lap, and as grown men. They had suffered greatly from the loss of their Mummy. Actually they had never got over it.

'She would have done better to stay with her children,' said my mother. 'What was there for her on a ship like that? But well, she wanted to take it easy. Women who want to take it easy had better not have children.'

Yes, Mummy.

She never set foot in a beauty salon.

Perhaps it would have been better if she had.

Shame on you, Odette! I don't want to hear that kind of thing again! What a cheek!

Sorry, Mummy. It won't happen again, Mummy.

I thought she was so ugly. Even with her most chic silk scarf and her Chanel lipstick and her Lancôme powder and her diamond earrings—a present from my father on their tenth wedding anniversary—I thought she was ugly. And I think she knew. I couldn't keep anything secret from her.

She would have done better not to tart herself up. It made her uglier.

Who did she do it for?

God rest her soul. Died while her daughter was in prison, and was loathed by the whole country. The fruit of her womb. *Le fruit de ses entrailles. La pauvre.*

They buried her next to my father. Her name and date of birth had been carved in the tombstone for over thirty years. And there was also room for me, she said. I bet she was counting on dragging me into that grave with her. If she had had the chance, she would have done it.

I don't know if I want to go there. I don't need to go. I can see that grave in my dreams, I've been there so often. Week in, week out.

There are so many other things I want to do. Especially with the children, if they want to. Please let them want to. All those lost years!

Don't think about it, Odette. Don't think about it.

What I'd most like to do is sit on a bench in a park. Feel the sun and the wind. Hear the birds sing. Watch the ducks on the water. Forget prison exists. And go to the seaside, to the seaside, to the seaside. Stroll along the promenade. Dance.

M was a good dancer. That came from skating, he said. 'All good skaters are good dancers.'

He didn't think that I was a good dancer, or a good

skater, but I danced and skated better than his first wife. He thought I was prettier than her. I thought so too. Everyone thought so. He was afraid she would never find another man after him. He said, 'I can't leave her in the lurch, because otherwise she'll never get to fuck again. Do you know what that means to a woman of her age to realise that she will never fuck again? I can't do that to her.' He organised a special party for her to which he invited all the bachelors he knew. And they had to bring the bachelors they knew. He acted as DJ. He had never done it before, but he did it very well. He played only bambas and slow romantic numbers. And he gave free beers to anyone who danced with his wife. While she had no one else, he felt responsible for her. He told me that immediately, on the very day we met. I realised that I had to take her as part of the package. And that I was lucky not to have to take his mother as well. Some men demanded that, he said, but I could treat him as if he had no mother. Or father either.

I can't say even approximately how often the three of us went out together, I and his first wife, and I often looked after her children, his children too, and then there was Sasha-with-the-fur-hat, until I was really sick, absolutely sick of it, and then he gave that party to find a new man for his first wife.

It was a bit embarrassing for her. Everyone knew why M was giving the party. And his friends felt obliged to dance with her. She wasn't stupid, was she? She was only too aware. She would have preferred everything to stay as it was.

Not me.

We went together to buy clothes for her. He almost never came up with any money, on this occasion he did. He realised that something had to happen. He had even sent her to the optician for prescription contact lenses, but she couldn't wear them. She claimed they made her eyes sting. 'You'll get used to them,' I said. 'No,' she said. She could be very stubborn. You wouldn't have thought her capable of it, but she was. The worst thing was that she could not return the lenses to the optician, or the products she had bought. All money down the drain.

She had been an orphan for years and years. No one had taught her how to make herself presentable. She wouldn't have learnt it from the nuns in the orphanage.

She and I must have tried twenty shops before we found something that was sexy, but not vulgar or ridiculous. We get home and she puts it on, and I make up her eyes dramatically, so that even with those glasses on her nose they are still seen to their best advantage. I give her my lipstick and she makes up her lips in front of the mirror, and she runs her tongue over her lips, and suddenly I see M looking at her, and I think: help, soon he'll want to keep her.

Because she had something. Not at first sight, but when you got to know her better, and if you could picture her without those glasses... If I'm really honest, I have to admit I can see what M saw in her.

We would have done better to buy some new frames for her. She would have had years of pleasure from them.

She was determined to buy shoes with heels and those fine straps, but she wasn't used to them. In the end she danced in her bare feet. At the beginning of the evening she kept changing partners, but after a while she danced with the same one the whole time. I breathed a sigh of relief.

Here in prison there is also dancing sometimes, but I don't join in. Women dancing with women are almost as pathetic as women having sex with women. That was different with Sasha and me. We wouldn't have touched each other without a man present. We did it for M. We knew it excited him. *That* was our aim.

If I ever dance again, I will dance alone. Or with a man. A real man who gets an erection when he dances with me. Like that man at the party for M's first wife. 'Nights in white satin, never reaching the end.' It went on and on. 'Cause I love you, yes I love you, oh how I love you, oh how I love you...' And the whole time I felt that thing between us, and I thought: M will kill him. If he knows what that guy has in his trousers, he'll kill him. And me too. I didn't dare leave him standing in the middle of the dance floor. That would really have drawn attention to us. When the number finally finished I made it clear as discreetly as possible that I had had enough. Then I joined M at the mixing desk. He said nothing about the man, but he trod on my toes, without saying anything. He didn't have to say anything.

Sometimes I think that I think of those murderess-mothers in order not to think of him for ten minutes.

When two people think of each other over an extended period, in such a way that they think of nothing else, they can read each other's thoughts. No, no, they actually read each other's thoughts. If you happen to cross the line running between their brains you get an electric shock, as if you are a cow bumping into the electrified fence around its field.

I'm not a cow.

I'm not in a field.

No one has ever milked me. Not even M.

It must have slipped out.

Sorry for laughing. A woman like me has no right to laugh, but I can see the line of bottles in which he would have collected my milk for customers male and female. To think he never thought of that! That could have been profitable.

Yesterday someone in the canteen said that in London there's an ice-cream parlour where you can get ice cream made from mother's milk. I had never seen her before. She hadn't seen me either, but she knew who I was, because she stared at me with cow's eyes, very soon they would be rolling out of their sockets. The new ones are always full of stories, they think we in here don't know anything about what's happening outside. I didn't ask her name, otherwise she might get the idea she interested me. I just wanted to know everything about that mother's milk ice cream. Apparently it's a great success. Since they put it on the menu, sales have doubled. The whole of London wants mother's milk ice cream. Not just cheeky young guys trying to act tough, no, no, older people too. Mothers buy it for their children, and for themselves. I refused to believe it, but Anouk said that it's true. There are even people who travel to London especially to taste that ice cream, although it costs three times as much as normal ice cream. They think it's healthy. That it protects them against cancer. And that it will make their skin as soft as a baby's.

'That's disgusting,' I said.

'Why?' asked Anouk.

'That milk is for babies. You don't steal babies' food because you feel like an ice cream.'

Her mouth dropped open, but the words stuck in her

throat. She blinked and got red blotches on her neck. In a moment she'll explode, I thought. I knew what she was thinking. I'm not backward. She's lumping everything together. She's too stupid to see the difference. Sometimes I wonder which of us studied psychology. People with a university degree think they know it all. They sit on their little island and they believe they know the world. They see nothing, they hear nothing. All they see and hear is themselves.

When M heard the ice cream van, he hunted in his pockets for money. Or he took it from Gilles' piggy bank. Or out of my bag. No notes, but coins. Ice cream had to be paid for with coins. Then it seemed cheaper. Everything you could pay for with coins was cheap. If he was in a good mood he paid with a note to get change. That was for the extras, the treats, the ice creams. If he was in a bad mood, it was exactly the other way round. And God help me if I had no coins for his ice cream. Or if there were no coins in Gilles's piggy bank.

He always had two scoops: chocolate and mocha. And if they had no mocha: chocolate and coffee. Or pistachio. Or banana. He liked those too. There was always chocolate. Like vanilla. Gilles was always allowed to have a lick. 'A whole ice cream is too much for a child. And bad for their teeth.' He would never have tried mother's milk ice cream. He would have thought it distasteful, I think, and would have been frightened of growing breasts. Some breast-fed babies grow breasts or menstruate a tiny bit. A friend of mine once found drops of blood in her son's nappy. She was in a panic, but the doctor said that it was a kind of period. And that it was actually perfectly normal. Mother's milk is full of female hormones: boys become girls for a moment.

Just imagine that happening with adults too.

M menstruating, having to wear a sanitary towel. And me with a penis. Not one of those strap-on dildos, but a real penis. One that has erections and can penetrate and come.

I should have forced him face down and fucked him in the arse like he did with me. Not with my fingers, but with a dildo. Or with the handle of a spoon or a screwdriver. I could have done it together with Sasha.

Women are much stronger than they think. Certainly if they cooperate. If they join forces.

Says Anouk.

'Find the energy in yourself, feel it, use it.'

She closes her eyes. We are her sheep that goggle at her. One always starts bleating. Hisses urge her to be quiet. The woman bleats more loudly, tears run down her cheeks, not tears of pain but tears of laughter. She crosses her legs and grabs her cunt. Everything in her goes limp, soon she'll be wetting herself. A sheep pissing with pleasure. Anouk pretends not to hear. Perhaps she really doesn't hear it. Energy streams and churns in her. That's all she hears.

Sometimes I think she's right.

I *am* stronger than I think.

I go and stand right behind him while he's peeing in the garden, prick in hand, insignificant little prick, I spread my legs slightly, plant my feet firmly next to his and hook my arms through his. I push my pelvis against his. He can't move.

He would have shaken me off like a fly. A gnat.

Does Anouk really think that he would have allowed himself to be overpowered by me?

M never tasted my milk. Perhaps he licked up a few

drops at some point. But he never suckled. I would remember something like that. His mother had not breast-fed him. Typical of her, but he didn't regret it. Nipples didn't interest him. Nor did cunts. 'Whether it's your cunt,' he said, 'or someone else's doesn't matter to me.' Did I know how many cunts there were on earth? Usable cunts? And how many mouths, usable mouths? How many arses? Had I ever tried to work it out?

Men's arses or women's arses, or arses in general? *En général.*

I didn't ask him that.

They maintain that years ago he let himself be fucked by a paedophile for money, but who can say if that's true? Perhaps it was M who did the fucking and the paedophile who was fucked. Those journalists write with great aplomb, as if they were present. And they call him a 'bum boy'. M won't find that funny. At any rate he never breathed a word about it to me, or about the gay who let M stay with him when his mother had driven him out of her house with her behaviour, or the other gay who is supposed to have met him at the gate of the factory where he worked. If you are to believe them, all the gays in Charleroi were after him. And he let them come after him and mess around with him.

I don't say these are lies, but nor do I say they're the truth.

He was wandering around at the time. His mother had a new lover with whom she was banging away all night. 'That doesn't work,' he said, 'a son who has to lie in bed listening to his mother making love.' It wasn't even a proper bed, but a camp bed. The beds had stayed at his father's. His father could sleep in a different bed every night if he wanted. The mother had run away with her children without taking anything with her.

When she needed anything, she sent him and his brother to get it, but they couldn't really cart away a whole bed. They knew the house well. They had lived there for years. They actually enjoyed breaking in.

These were his first thefts, on his mother's orders.

'*Mon père est un con.*' A bastard, who marched his own son to the mayor for breaking into his house. M had not let himself be caught. His brother did, being always slower-witted than M.

The mayor quickly threw him out of his office. Off with you! And give your children a little care and attention!

But meanwhile M had to try to get to sleep on a camp bed every night while his mother was in full cry in the room next door.

The lover was only three years older than M.

'She was winding me up,' he said. 'And so was he. During the day he was friendly and correct, but at night he wound me up. I had to get away.'

At that time M. looked younger than his age. So they write. That's why that paedophile fell for him, although he was already seventeen. It was a big frustration for M. that he did not look older and tougher. He wanted to make an impression on girls, but it was mainly paedos who were attracted.

Loser.

People also put me down as younger than I was. They still do. 'If I didn't know better I'd put you at forty,' says Anouk. I'm lucky with my hair. It gives me a youthful look. And she says she admires me because I don't let myself go. In a prison that demands great willpower.

I think she means it.

The only thing that interested M was his penis, an ice cream that sperm came out of. 'Swallow it,' he said, 'Just swallow it.'

It stuck in my throat like slime, or snot. Glue. My throat gummed up. I'm choking, I thought. I gagged.

I know it wasn't respectful, but I was frightened I was going to choke. It *was* slime, but I mustn't say that. And I wasn't allowed to spit it out. Sasha didn't spit it out. Nor did his first wife. Sasha thought his sperm was more delicious than oysters.

Oh yes? I had never tasted oysters, and afterwards I definitely no longer wanted to try them. They call them a treat, a delicacy.

Where and when had Sasha tasted oysters?

If I loved him, he said, I must love everything about him. If I didn't love everything I didn't really love him. That's why he washed so little. He wanted a woman who loved him, even his sweat, even when he stank.

Then I was afraid he would force me to swallow his piss. What is the difference between sperm and piss?

His penis was an ice cream, he said. 'You like licking ice creams, don't you.'

And now I sometimes wonder whether that paedophile said that to him. Perhaps he bought ice creams for M and one ice cream led to another.

I had to practise with a banana or a cucumber in order to develop my jaw muscles, or with a dildo. The stronger my jaw muscles were, the easier I could suck him off. Eventually it would be child's play. The whores in Charleroi gave twenty blow-jobs a day, or thirty. They didn't make a fuss about it. Why was I making a fuss? 'Practise,' he said, 'practise, practise, practise.'

And what about the bum boys? How many men did they give blow jobs a day?

They should develop a machine for it. To think that no one has yet had the idea!

One day he stood there with a box of oysters under his arm. M buying oysters! For me! They'd been reduced, but they were oysters. Twelve oysters from Zeeland. But it wasn't about me of course, it was about him. Once I had got the knack with oysters, it would work with sperm. 'You must let them slide down inside, Odette. You swallow them without tasting them.'

All the oysters were shut tight. You couldn't prise them open even with a screwdriver. It ended with him smashing them one by one with a hammer. And there was I praying: please don't let him bash my head.

I'd rather drop dead than eat an oyster. And I don't want sperm in my mouth ever again. Afterwards he gave me a piece of chocolate to get rid of the taste, a taste which according to him didn't exist. Sperm, he maintained, was colourless, odourless and tasteless, like oysters. Why do people want to eat oysters if you must let them slide down inside without tasting them? And why must you let them slide down inside if they taste of nothing?

He refused to try it himself. 'Come on,' I said, 'we'll catch it in a spoon and you can taste it. We'll add some lemon juice and some pepper and salt, and then you can tuck into your own sperm.'

Did I ever say that?

Of course not: I'd be six feet under if I'd said that.

I'm eyeballing him. He is blinking, I am not. I am wearing the blouse that Sasha gave me. A dud purchase, she called it, but maybe I would have use for it.

That was good thinking.

The blouse is buttoned in such a way that you can see

the start of my cleavage. It forms the ideal packaging for my breasts. Yet I shall shortly be taking them out of that packaging. I am still looking him straight in the eye. I take hold of the blouse just above where the blouse is buttoned, and also my bra. With a jerk I pull them both down. He bends towards me, closes his lips around my nipple and sucks.

I bare my other breast. He lets go of one nipple, and now sucks on the other. He moves to and fro between the two nipples.

Soon, I think, I will grab his penis. When I feel like it, I will grab it.

I must stop thinking about him.

He doesn't exist anymore, he doesn't exist anymore, he doesn't exist anymore.

He can't do anything to me anymore.

M isn't thinking of me.

M is thinking of M.

Once he said to me: 'I want love. It's your job to give me love. I can get sex from other women.' Why the hell didn't I give him love? Couldn't I see how he was suffering?

'But I give you love, every day. You don't see it. You can't see it. Or feel it. Love doesn't interest you.'

'You're a bad woman. You seduced me with lies and now you're destroying me. I had a good wife, a wife who loved me. You made me leave her. I should never have left her. Why should I have left her? She loved me. She looked after me. I never needed to ask her for anything. She gave it to me before I realised I needed it. How did you lure me away from her?

What did you make me drink? Witch, you're a witch, an enchantress. Before I knew you I never had problems with the police. I never raped anyone then. I didn't dream of it. You, you planted those thoughts in my head. I would never have done it. I didn't need to do it. Did I have to rape you? Or Sasha? Or my first wife? I'm not a rapist. Rapists are suckers. They can't get a woman in the normal way. I can. You made me into a rapist. How could I be so blind, so stupid, so foolish. It's all clear to me now. How did you manage it? You put something in my food. Is that it? Don't dare try to bewitch me again. I've seen through your tricks. I shall destroy you before you have the chance to destroy me. Have you got that?'

The longer he went on, the more energy he acquired. Like a battery charging up. Sometimes he calmed down for a moment, and if I was idiotic enough to ask if he was feeling better, he launched back into his tirade. He was inexhaustible. Eventually there was nothing left of me. Just a pool of sweat, urine, saliva. Something that could be wiped up with a mop.

There was poison in him. He had to be able to spew it out. If he hadn't spewed it out, it would have eaten him up.

And each time I thought: it's all out now. But then it began again. Sometimes the trigger was trivial, sometimes it was substantial, sometimes there was no trigger. It was unpredictable.

3

When I was pregnant with Gilles, I had a book of first names, pages and pages full of them, each with a short explanation of the meaning and origin. I had been given it by a friend. She felt she had enough children and gave away everything connected with pregnancy and babies, even her breast-feeding bra. She didn't want anything in the house that reminded her of her pregnancies, except for her children. She acted as if she had bought them in a supermarket, or found them under a gooseberry bush, or won them in the lottery. Before they started having children, she and her husband had put a budget aside for her to repair the damage caused after her last pregnancy. She said that literally: the damage caused. She had renewed her whole wardrobe and changed her hairstyle, and she went twice a week to fitness classes. You'll have to do that too, she said with a not very subtle look at my pregnant belly. And I should look for work. It wasn't good for a young mother to be always cooped up at home.

She had found work in Nivelles two streets away from the school where she and I had done our primary school teacher training. While she was teaching, her two eldest children would be in nursery classes at the same school, and a child minder would look after the baby. Children, she said, suffer more from a depressive mother than from an absent one. As soon as a vacancy came up at the school, she would tip me off. She seemed to assume that I would drop everything, as I had done in the past when we had to complete assignments together or prepare presentations. Or when she felt like a party and had persuaded my mother to let her invite the whole class to our place for a raclette dinner party. She had fixed it behind my back with my mother, without my knowing a thing. 'Didn't you say your mother could make such delicious raclette? Well, I felt like raclette! And she said that I was exaggerating. My mother wasn't at all amorphous, as I maintained. On the contrary, she found her bubbly and vital.

Bubbly and vital.

We got a child's high chair from her, and a wooden walking bike, and Barbie dolls. What was our Gilles supposed to do with Barbie dolls? He dyed their hair and cut it off, and later the dogs chewed them up. Bye bye Barbie dolls.

When M was in prison for the first time, she dropped by unannounced a few times with hand-me-downs from her children, but also from herself. There were some nice things among them, without much wear. And I could always ring her if I needed anything. She needed people to need her. I called her often and on a few occasions she was a big help, until I landed in jail myself. Then I didn't hear from her anymore.

It was probably a shock to her.

A lot of people were shocked at the time.

I was too. I was even more shocked when I read in my

file all the things that that so-called friend told the police about me. I never left Gilles alone in order to go out. Ever!

What mother leaves a nine-month-old baby in his cot to go flirting with other men? *She* wanted to get away from her children. She felt shut in as a mother at home. I didn't. I had no need for other men. I didn't need to seduce men by showing them a porn video. Where did she get that from? I told her, she claimed. Oh yes? When? How? Why? I had a man. If I wanted, I could have sex three times a day with him, or five times. He was a real man. He didn't need Viagra. I sometimes watched porn with him, true. What else are those porn movies for? But I never watched porn with M's friends. Unless M was there. Sometimes he liked having me there. Sometimes he didn't. I adapted, as I expect she also adapted to her husband. If you want a relationship to last, you have to adapt. Compromise, not always wanting to have your cake and eat it.

I'll ring up her husband sometime and spill the beans about her. It will be a long telephone conversation.

Raclette dinner party! We all know why she wanted a raclette dinner party with the whole class. 'No sweethearts, just the class!' And by pure coincidence the table was arranged so that she was sitting opposite Antoine with the raclette grill between them. But she couldn't get him, of course. He was gay, as it turned out later.

Why did she have to come and play the vamp at my house of all places?

We didn't tell her husband at the time. They weren't yet married, but they had been together for three years. He worked in a law office. If she needed something copied, she got him to do it. The lawyers' photocopier worked flat out for her. That's theft, isn't it? Isn't it theft?

Then she breezed in with a Delvaux bag under her arm, while my husband was in prison and I was on sick benefit, and had been declared disabled. She always wanted me to look for work, but I couldn't work. I was unfit for work and I was receiving sick benefit. But she knew better than all those doctors and psychiatrists put together.

Her children were called Aymeric, Anémone and Arielle.

Très chic.

She had never got any further in that book than the A.

And God help you if you abbreviated Aymeric to Aymé or Ric!

Her children will probably have left home by now. Perhaps they have children of their own. And Antoine is married to a man. He sent me an invitation with a covering note to say that he knew I couldn't come, but that he wanted to let me know anyway. He was one of the first gays to get married. That is one of the things I will have to get used to, says Anouk. Now men can marry men and women marry women. They are just as married as M and I ever were. I hope for them that they can also get divorced. I really hope so.

In that book there were names I had never heard of and which I definitely didn't want to lumber a child with. Names that weren't names at all, in my view. I wanted traditional French names, which could be easily pronounced and weren't too difficult to spell. And which wouldn't make the children a laughing stock. Aymeric, for example, is too difficult, I think. But they mustn't be hackneyed names either. Traditional but still original, that was my ideal. Anémone, for example, is not bad. I wouldn't have minded calling my daughter Anémone. Or Anouk, only I would spell it with ck. Or Odette. But children mustn't have the same names as their parents. Fortunately I didn't opt for Geneviève. I would hate that now. The name was on my list for a long time. I think it even made the top ten. But the final choice was Elise, as in *Für Elise*.

A strong name, I said, is a strong start.

In that respect M had not been given a strong start. In other respects too. His parents obviously saw things differently, because when a year later a second child was born, they gave him the same names, but in a different order. With the third son they dusted off the three names again, once more in a different order. I wouldn't let M try that on with our children, and he didn't try.

It didn't interest him. I could have numbered them, as the Romans did. At first I thought he was pulling my leg, but it's true. The Romans gave their children not names but numbers. Not all Romans did it, but some called their children Primus, Secundus, Tertius, Quartus, Quintus, Sextus, etc. Primus. That's a brand of gas canisters, and beer. M was capable of calling our son Primus to needle me. And the next one Heineken and the third Stella, with the same middle name of Skol, or Santé. Hahaha!

A name is a name is a name, he said. Why did I make such a big fuss about it? But meanwhile he wanted to change his own name. Not his first name, but his surname. 'They've got it in for me,' he said. 'They're looking for me.' With a different name they wouldn't be able to find him as easily. He could have started by buying a less garish van. If he had put a flashing light on the roof, it couldn't have stood out more. I told him a hundred times that he should take off those stickers at the back, and replace those filthy curtains. You could hear him coming miles away in that rust heap. 'Have the van resprayed,' I said. 'Or do it yourself. You can do it, can't you?' And I said he should pay more attention to his appearance. They would go on treating him like a criminal, because he looked like a criminal. 'You should wash your hair more often. I bought shampoo for greasy hair especially for you, but you've never used it yet. Shave that beard off. Wear a shirt. Go to the barber. Cut your nails.' He pretended not to hear me, or he thought I was nagging. How dare I criticise him, when he toiled day and night for his family? Did I want him to drop dead on the job? Would I be happy then? Sometimes he began counting, and if I hadn't stopped before he got to three...

If one of us nagged, it was him. About those canisters of butane gas, for instance, for which they had searched his place. It was nothing to do with me, it was before my time, but again and again he made out it was *me* who had wound up the police. If I had been friendlier, they would have left him in peace. I should have offered them a beer, I should have kept them talking. I should have given them a friendly smile, shown a bit of cleavage, but no, I behaved as if I had something to hide, and so those slobs used their search warrant. He should have snatched it out of their hands. He should have torn it up under their noses. He had taken those canisters of butane gas, yes, on the assumption that someone had put them there to get rid of them. He had taken them to the steelworks, where they were melted down. Scrap metal merchants like him kept the streets and squares clean. 'They should have paid us instead of fining us. That was ecology *avant la lettre*!'

His problem was that he was too honest. So honest that he had paid for all the hi-fi towers and car radios and recording equipment they found in his house. Or he had obtained them from someone who had paid for them. But those fucking policemen didn't believe that. They wanted to see receipts and invoices. Who on earth keeps an invoice for every purchase? He was given a three-month suspended sentence for two empty gas canisters that he had 'stolen' by mistake. Had those guys fallen on their heads? It was a perversion of justice. And it was my fault that he had been unjustly sentenced. And afterwards had grown bitter about it. If I hadn't been so jumpy, they wouldn't have searched his house. He would have stayed on the straight and narrow. I, I had been his undoing.

I shouted that I didn't even know him then. His hand rose in the air. One, two... I could have some more if I wanted. Christ Almighty!

Quiet, Odette. Let him let off steam. It'll blow over.

He felt victimised, although afterwards everyone was convinced that he had protection from on high.

If only that had been true!

In order to change his surname he needed his father's permission, just as he did when he got married for the first time. On that occasion he needed permission from both his parents because he was under twenty-five. That is what the law required in those days. His mother hit on the bright idea of fooling the police into believing that his father had vanished without trace and so *couldn't* give permission. Later M admitted that to his father in all honesty and wham, the father brought a charge against him! Result: a sentence for forging a document *and* a criminal record. For M, not for his mother, though it was she who didn't want the father at the wedding. She wanted to be able to flaunt her new man. Her young lover. Her trophy, her toy boy. She had egged M on. But M was sentenced.

M's problem was that he had played fair and square. He should have lied, about those gas canisters too. Honesty gets you nowhere. But he didn't want to lie because his mother had always lied to him. He was sick of her lies. He wanted to prove it could be done differently, but it couldn't.

M wasn't a liar. He did not always tell the whole truth, but he didn't tell lies. He never led me to expect a monogamous relationship. 'I need more than one woman,' he said.

That family! What father gives his son a criminal record? Later his mother also brought an action against him, because he wanted to protect *her* mother against her. M loved his Granny. He thought the world of her. But she... He wanted to sever the links with his parents. That's why he wanted to change his name.

'It's my name,' said M. 'I'll do what I like with it.'

It wasn't to be.

They know that name all over the world now, and they spit it out.

Lhermitte is not spat out. Geneviève Lhermitte, a perfectly ordinary Belgian name. Less ordinary than mine, but ordinary enough not to make the lives of all the other Lhermittes impossible. Which unfortunately cannot be said of M's namesakes. His name is ripe for the dustbin. And that while his father was so proud of it. He talked as if he came from a noble family, and his grandparents' home was a country estate. The Lords of B. The year of construction was carved in a beam above the hearth. Seventeen hundred and sixty-eight. Twenty-one years before the French Revolution. As a child he had often looked at it. And he said we should all make an excursion to the farm. He hadn't been there for ages. I must see where the roots were of the family I had married into. As if I were Mathilde marrying the heir to the throne. Princess Odette of Belgium.

Mehdi. That was what Lhermitte's youngest was called. The little chap was only three. The only son after four girls in a row. Yasmine, Nora, Myriam, Mina and then Mehdi. They must have looked for names that sounded both Arabic and Belgian. Except for Mehdi. The father probably said: my son will be given an Arab name. End of story.

With M it was exactly the reverse: first four sons, two with his first wife, two with me. Then the long-awaited daughter, to whom he subsequently paid no attention. Did I expect it to be otherwise? Yes and no. I knew he was under enormous pressure. He had told me all about the stupid things he and his mates had got up to, and about which I did not want to hear a word. It didn't concern me at all. But he couldn't stand that. *He* wanted things to be like they used to be between us, when we discussed everything from a to z and I went everywhere with him, for adventure. I had enough of his adventures. He accused me of having changed. Of course I had changed. I had spent two years in prison for my part in his adventures. Which he had often forced me into by sticking a revolver against my temples. He had obviously forgotten that 'detail', and the police took no account of it either.

I returned from prison in poor health after two years. They classified me as sixty-six per cent disabled because of chronic depression. M had no consideration for my condition. He treated me as his slave. He demanded food, he demanded sex. At a certain moment he took it into his head that the roof of one of his houses should be raised, the house that had been a farm and that we often called 'the farm'. Later he was to dump me in it as a tenant with the children. Making me pay rent, me, his own wife and the mother of his children. For now it was standing empty. It had to be higher, because then it was worth more. But of course he didn't want to pay anyone to do the work. Why should he pay someone when he had free labour? So I had to climb up and down a steep ladder like a construction worker with roof tiles on my shoulder, when I was disabled and pregnant. With my dear darling Jérôme. I was so frightened of losing him. I didn't want a second miscarriage. I didn't even take my pills for depression any more. The doctor said a low dose wouldn't hurt, but I didn't want to take any risks. Anything, but not that emptiness again, that sense of loss, that hole in my body and in my heart.

It had happened while I was on remand, three years before the actual prison sentence, which was to last two years. They had torn Gilles out of my arms, just as eleven years later they were to tear Elise out of my arms, and they had thrown me into prison on remand, WHILE I WAS PREGNANT. Why was that necessary? In what other country do they put pregnant women in prison, on remand or not? I was given a curettage. In prison. 'We'll look after you,' they said. I mustn't be afraid, they would look after me properly, as well as in an ordinary hospital. They maintained that the baby had been dead for two months. It was dead in my womb.

Lies they told in order to obscure their part in the death of my child. M was furious. He wanted to make an official complaint and I found it hard to argue with him. It was *his* child too. Some women are made ill by the child they have, but I was made ill by the child I had lost. M suffered from that too. No one ever took account of our feelings, ever. We had no right to feelings. We have no right to feelings.

I had learned my lesson; he had not. With him things went from bad to worse. Much worse. So bad that I didn't want to know about it. I didn't want to hear a word about it.

The man was mad. And he drove me mad.

By this time M and I were no longer living together. I had my house, he had his. That was the best solution for us both because of our benefit payments. M had worked out that in this way we were both eligible for the highest possible amount. He dropped round to eat or deliver his laundry or for sex, but they were two separate households. I paid him rent, because all the houses were his. They were in his name and had been paid for by him. As soon as he had any money, he bought a house. As if he were playing monopoly. Often it was no more than a squat or a hovel.

Officially Gilles lived with him, but in reality the children and the dogs were with me, on the farm. In that way M could do what he liked at home and I needn't know. But I knew anyway. He couldn't keep quiet about it. With me he couldn't. He had to tell someone, otherwise he would go crazy. I had no one to whom I could pour out my heart. I had to keep my mouth shut. Keep silent as the grave.

He used me as a dustbin for his filthy tricks. I did not

want to listen to them and I couldn't listen to them. I had two children and I was pregnant again. This time with Elise. I pretended to listen, but meanwhile I sang a song in my head. 'In Lourdes in the mountains there appeared in a cave, shining and glorious the mother of God. Ave, Ave, Ave Maria! Oh when the saints go marching in...' The gynaecologist had prescribed rest, lots of rest, otherwise the baby would be born prematurely. Perhaps I would lose her. No miscarriage, please, no miscarriage.

His first wife had warned me: don't get involved with children. Don't make the same mistake as I did. As soon as he knows you're pregnant you won't recognise him anymore. He's a child himself. He's worse than a child. He wants all the attention for himself.

That was true.

But he also wanted children. He really wanted them.

He longed for the cosiness of a family.

He wanted everything.

It was never enough.

Egoist. Fat, filthy, dirty egoist.

Who suffered most from it himself.

He too had expected it to be different. After all those years there was a daughter and he felt nothing. Rage is what he felt, and self-pity because he did not feel any of the things a father was supposed to feel. 'It's hell,' he sometimes said. 'Not feeling anything is hell.' And could I please release him from that hell.

If only I had been able!

'Allow yourself a little time,' I said soothingly.

I could see he was shattered. He couldn't sit still for a moment. I tried to put Elise in his arms, but he pushed her away. Hadn't I heard what he had said to me? No, because I didn't want to hear! He had bought a mobile home, he said. I liked the idea of a mobile home, didn't I? Well, he had bought one. It needed some work, but the five of us could go out in it. Wasn't I happy?

'Yes,' I said. 'I'm happy. *Je suis heureuse.*'

But I didn't want to listen to his bad news. I didn't want to know how he had got rid of W. I prayed it wasn't true. Was the father of my children a murderer? It couldn't be true. He was exaggerating. He was confused. Perhaps W had had an accident and he was presenting it as if he was responsible. Perhaps he felt guilty because he had not been able to prevent the accident. Or he was presenting it as a murder to make himself look important in my eyes—or in his own eyes.

Everything was possible.

His hands and nails were dirty. God knows where he had been all that time.

'Her name's Elise,' I said, as if she had been born with a name tag round her wrist.

He didn't react.

'Don't you want to know how it went?' I asked.

'I want to know why I wasn't allowed to be there. You were going to beep me. Why didn't you beep me?'

The midwife had asked me. 'Shall we wait for your husband?' I was already having contractions. Did she plan to push a cork in me until 'hubbie' showed up? And now hubbie was angry. I should have beeped him.

'I rang you.'

'And I asked you to beep me when she was about to be born.'

'How was I supposed to beep you?'

'Are you really soft in the head, Odette, or are you pretending to be?'

'Do you like the name?'

'It's a name.'

He went over to the window. Suddenly he turned and went out of the room.

'He does love you,' I said to Elise. 'He's bought a mobile home especially for you. To celebrate your coming into the world. Perhaps we'll drive all the way to Spain. Or Italy. Or to Germany. Or Switzerland. But not to Slovakia, because Daddy sometimes goes there to... Don't think of that, don't think of that. There are lots of countries we can drive to, lots and lots. Your Daddy at the wheel and me next to him with the map. You and your brothers mustn't make too much noise or your Daddy will get angry. Or nervous. Or both. And I won't be able to look after you, because I'll have to watch the road, and the map and give your father a piece of chocolate occasionally, as he needs lots of energy when he's driving. Mummies often have to divide their attention between their children and the Daddy of those children. But first we're going to give a baby shower for you. And we'll write on the invitation that you want things that are for girls. You've got enough for boys from your brothers, but you're not a boy. You're a girl. And then everyone will be able to see how beautiful you are. You're my dolly, and I'm going to dress you like a doll. Oh, you're hungry again. Do you want to feed again? Come on, Mummy has lovely milk for you.'

I daren't think what had happened to W. And I daren't think about the girls in the cellar either. It was impossible, absolutely impossible. Positive thinking. That's what it said in the booklet on breast feeding. Avoid stress. That was easier said than done. But I wanted to try. I had to try. Not for myself, for Elise.

Before we had children, M and I sometimes pretended the van was a mobile home and that we were driving round America in it. We wore the Stetsons M had picked up somewhere and put on a tape of country music. 'Country roads, take me home…!' We fantasised that we were on our way to a gig in Nashville and that we were going to spend the night there. 'Stand by your man, give him two arms to cling to. Jolene, Jolene, Jolene, I'm begging of you please don't take my man.' I loved it. Sometimes it brought tears to my eyes. 'Please don't take him just because you can.'

'If you want, we can fly to America tomorrow,' M said in a macho tone. I knew we wouldn't be flying to America. But he said it as if he meant it. And he did mean it. He meant it at that moment. And he felt like a man. And he *was* a man. Calm. Strong. Full of confidence. He said it was easier to carry out a robbery in America than here. Everyone committed robberies over there. 'People here are scared,' he said. 'Everything's there for the taking, but they don't dare take it.'

'They're stupid,' I said. 'Ugly and stupid.' With a shudder I thought of my mother, who had intended to tie me to her until her death. And afterwards she would have dragged me down with her into her grave.

At moments like these I felt safe with him. And proud because he was my man. *Mon mec.* I knew he would never leave me. There would be other women, but I would always come first, I and the children. He wanted to provide for us, and actually he always did. Perhaps not as I would have liked, but he did it. He did it in his way.

When Elise was born he had just had to make sure W kept his mouth shut. He had given W a number of chances, but W was pig-headed. M had had no alternative. It weighed heavily on him. It weighed on him every second of the day and night. But he did not use that as an excuse. He continued to take responsibility towards me and the children.

When it looked as if Elise would soon be arriving, he had taken Jérôme to my mother in Waterloo. He parked Gilles with an old sweetheart of his. I had agreed to this. My mother couldn't handle looking after two children and we couldn't rely on his family. I don't call them family. Family are there for each other. Family come to visit when a baby has just been born, with a present or with flowers. And they ask if they can do anything to help.

After his lightning visit to the hospital, I heard nothing more from him for two days. No phone call, nothing. Suddenly he was back, with sunglasses and a Chevron basketball cap. He came to collect us. It was nine in the morning and the doctors had not yet done their rounds. I was still entitled to three days' rest in the hospital, but no, we had to go with him. I scarcely had time to pack my things. It was raining hard and we had no umbrella or raincoat, but he refused to wait. I must simply hug Elise close to me, he said. A bit of rain would toughen her up.

He knew that the police could arrest him at any moment because he had yet again driven off in cars or trucks that were not his. His lordship couldn't stop, his lordship felt he had a right to them. *Soit.* If he went to jail, he had a serious problem. W had not been his only problem. There was another problem, one that could not be solved so easily. It wasn't my problem. I didn't have to find a solution. Burn your bum, and you have to live with the blisters. He had burnt his bum, not me. I had to look after my baby. And Gilles and Jérôme.

We drove first to Waterloo to collect Jérôme, then we picked up Gilles and finally the dogs, which were with two different neighbours. I would have liked to stay longer at my mother's, but with M it was hurry, hurry, hurry. And the whole time he kept that stupid basketball cap and those sunglasses on, while it was raining outside. There wasn't even time for a photo of my mother with her youngest grandchild.

At about eleven he dropped us off in front of the farm. He did not even come in with us. There was nothing in the house, it was cold and chilly. How was I supposed to go shopping with three small children? I felt so tired, so tired, so tired. Why couldn't I stay in hospital any longer? Gilles was hungry. He had been given almost nothing to eat by that ex-sweetheart of his father's. The dogs were moving restlessly to and fro. There was pus leaking from Brutus's ear. Someone must take him to the vet. When and how? The pilot light in the geyser in the kitchen had gone out and I had no matches or a lighter. Jérôme wanted to hold the baby. I said: 'You'll drop her. Elise isn't a doll.' And I thought: she's my doll. I'll do what I like with her. I was frightened I would drop her. Not drop her, but smash her on the ground in order to be rid of her. To be rid of everything. I wanted to sleep. I wanted to take sleeping pills and never wake up, but I wasn't allowed to take sleeping pills. The doctor had told me. No sleeping medication while I was breast feeding.

I was losing blood and there were no sanitary towels in the house. While I was pregnant I hadn't needed them.

My mother would have helped me, but she was in Waterloo, and he did not want her to come to ours. She didn't want to either. Sometimes she came anyway, but she never stayed long, and moaned about the house being dirty. How could I live in that shit? What were all those wrecks doing in the garden?—'It's not a garden, Mum, it's a yard. There used to be pigs and chickens and cows. There was a smouldering, stinking, rotting dunghill.'—But why were there wrecks lying about? What was M planning to do with those wrecks? And why didn't I have a bathroom? It would soon be the twenty-first century and I was washing myself and the children at the sink in the kitchen. No wonder we were dirty. She was ashamed of being seen with us in the street, because we were dirtier than gypsies.

I'll strangle her, I sometimes thought. If I strangle her, she'll stop.

I was glad when she came, but after an hour we were at daggers drawn, sometimes after half an hour. My mother hated M. He was the worst thing that had happened to her, much worse than Dad's death.

I thought: I'll turn on the gas and sit on the sofa with the children and the dogs and wait until we are all dead.

Then I saw a number for a helpline next to the telephone. I called them and said I needed help. Somebody would have to do the shopping for me, otherwise my children and dogs would have nothing to eat. I don't know what would have happened if I hadn't seen that number lying there. I think God must have put it by the telephone. Or an angel.

He could have made sure there was food in the house when I came home with the baby, couldn't he? Was that too much to ask? He wanted a daughter. He had read in *Science & Vie* that sperm cells with an X chromosome live longer than those with a Y chromosome and so I had to go around with a condom full of sperm in my vagina. After forty-eight hours I had to prick a hole in the condom with a needle. The sperm cells with a Y chromosome would be dead, while those with an X chromosome would not. And it worked. I can recommend it to people who want a daughter. M is no fool, but when the gynaecologist had seen on the ultrasound that it was a girl, he didn't react. 'Don't you remember how you made me walk round with a condom inside me?' I asked. Silence. Indifference.

I think he'd forgotten.

I hadn't. He had used my belly as a laboratory for an experiment.

I distance myself from what some papers have written about the motives behind M's wishes for a daughter. You have to be sick to write things like that. That wouldn't even have occurred to me or M. And I hope and pray that Elise never sees them. The child has suffered enough. She has a right to a little peace and happiness, and so do I.

Don't cry, Odette. It exhausts you, it makes you ugly, it does no one any good. Not even Elise. She has seen her mother cry more than enough.

It's easy for Anouk to talk. She should go through it. Then she would know how you are throttled, sometimes by a hand, sometimes by fear, helpless, blind, insidious panicky fear. No, you're not being throttled, your throat swells up, everything swells up, so that you can't take any more air in. You choke.

Crocodile tears, they said when I cried for Lhermitte's children. And they said I didn't have the right to hang their photos in my cell. If I thought I could impress them like that! If I was hoping to be released earlier like that! Why didn't I cry for the children whose blood is on my hands?

Because there is no blood on my hands. They don't understand, and they never will understand. I don't even try to explain anymore.

I sat on my bed and let the beads of my rosary slip through my fingers. And I murmured the names of the five children that Lhermitte murdered: Yasmine, Nora, Myriam, Mina, Mehdi. Pray for them, pray for them, pray for them.

I didn't look at the door. If I didn't look, the voices would die away.

They died away.

I don't pray for the murderess-mothers. Not then and not now. I will never pray for them. And I don't pray for M either. I'm not a saint. I'm a monster.

They aren't.

In fact, people pity them. Poor women who were in such despair that they murdered their own children!

Whoever pitied me?

Pitié. Ayez pitié.

If ever I have another chance to choose a name for a child, I'll call it Ayezpitié. Or perhaps I'll call him Mehdi. And Mina for a girl.

No, Mina is a name for a cat. Mina the cat.

Gilles wants children. It was in the paper, so I expect it's true. Or not true. Then I'll become a Granny like my mother. They can call me Granny. *Grand-mère. Mamie. Bobonne. Marraine. Meme.* They're all fine. I shall be proud.

Perhaps Gilles will let me choose the name. A gift for you, Mum. Because you had to go without so much.

I won't baptise him Ayezpitié, but Dieumerci. Like that footballer they awarded the Golden Boot.

No one has ever given anything to me. A hiding, yes, I've had that.

Because I deserved it, said M.

He was right. He was always right.

Would I be allowed to keep a cat in the convent? Or a dog? A Jack Russell, for example? Or chickens, to be able to have fresh eggs every day? They used to grow all their own vegetables, says Sister Virginie, now it's just a little lettuce, tomatoes, courgettes and some herbs. Once they even had a pig, and goats. But livestock was too much trouble. Is too much trouble.

That is true.

4

I bet Lhermitte will be given something to calm her nerves. No shortage of pills in Belgium. We're a pill paradise, M said. Never go to the same doctor twice. Or at least let enough time elapse between visits so they don't remember what they prescribed the last time, or so they can't find the papers on which they made a note of it. What do they care anyway? The more pills they prescribe, the more they're showered with freebies by the pharmaceutical companies. That way everybody's happy.

A prescription here, a prescription there: slowly but surely you build up a supply, and you become independent of doctors and pharmacists.

'I could have been a doctor,' M often said. 'If I'd had the chance to go on studying, I could have been a doctor, or a surgeon. In the first year at primary school I was top of the class, with ninety-six marks out of a hundred. I deserved a hundred per cent, because I hadn't made a single mistake, but they didn't give a hundred per cent. There's no such thing as perfection, they claimed. But there *was*: I had already performed perfectly in all those exams.'

He said he was an ace at mental arithmetic. Sales assistants had better not try overcharging him. Long before he reached the till he had always worked out the total. Not with a calculator, no, no, with his brain. He was never wrong. The women at the checkout were, but he wasn't. You had to train your mind: with chess, with mental arithmetic, with intellectual gymnastics.

The times Gilles and I had to hear about that ninety-six per cent, and how unjust it was that they hadn't awarded him a hundred!

Later he had been sent to the wrong schools, he said, schools where he wasn't given a chance because his mother had blackened his name when she came to enrol him. She called him 'a creep'. What mother calls her son 'a creep'? Winter and summer, she forced him to go to school in short trousers. That would toughen him up, or maybe it was cheaper. How could he win respect in short trousers? His mother was jealous of him because he had brains, and she didn't. And she was jealous of his father too. His father and he were the chess players in the family. A little child knows that of all sports chess requires the highest IQ in its practitioners. His mother wasn't even capable of retaining how you positioned the pieces on the board. And so she humiliated him, and she humiliated his father too. First she married him because she looked up to him, and then she belittled him. She tried to make him as small as she was. That was typical female behaviour. Every man must be on his guard against it. He had seen it at home and had sworn to himself that it would not happen to him. God help me if I ever tried it with him.

It would have been better if he had been born stupid

like his brothers, the postmen; she wouldn't have thwarted him then. If she hadn't thwarted him, he would have become a doctor. Doctors were in charge of their own bodies. They never needed to buy medicines. They were given samples by the sackful, much more than they could use themselves. A quarter of all medicines produced disappeared into samples. What was he saying, a quarter? Half!

'You must ask for samples, Odette.'

He asked for samples everywhere, even when he bought paint, or glue, or maintenance and cleaning products. Eventually I did the same. I would go into a perfume shop and ask for samples, without buying anything. 'My daughter collects them,' I would say, and smile. It was important not to forget to smile.

M never smiled, but he was a man. He *is* a man, with a heart and a face of steel.

Never go twice to the same perfume shop. Don't go anywhere twice if you can avoid it. Make sure no one remembers your face.

It's even better to have no face at all.

The woman without a face, that's me. How I would like to be. And no, I don't want another face if I ever get out of here. I'm frightened of needles and operations. If they sedate you, you never know for sure when you'll wake up, and if you'll wake up, and what you've said, or done, under sedation.

Yesterday a journalist who has written a lot about M maintained that I had had my hair cut short and dyed to make myself unrecognisable. And that I was in touch with a plastic surgeon, who will operate on me as soon as I am released.

Pay no attention, says Anouk. The guy is trying to earn a crust. And she said I am lucky with my hair. Lots of women of my age would pay good money to have hair like mine. Was it my natural colour?

I didn't answer.

I find those remarks about my hair a bit wearisome. And somehow inappropriate.

My mother always went to the same hairdresser because the hairdresser knew her hair better than she did herself. 'She can tell from my hair how I'm feeling.' And if she wasn't feeling well, the hairdresser knew which product to treat my mother's hair with to revive it. That hairdresser had the knack. 'Look,' my mother sometimes said, 'my ends are splitting.' It was her way of saying she wasn't feeling well. When she had been to the hairdresser's, she usually felt a bit better.

She had a loyalty card. Once she had ten shampoo and sets on her card, she got the eleventh for half price. She had loyalty cards for all her favourite shops, so that after ten or fifteen or twenty purchases she got five, six or sometimes even ten percent off. She was given samples in all those shops because she was such a loyal customer. She didn't even have to ask for them. The assistants rummaged in the basket or tray and beamed as they put a handful of samples on top of my mother's purchases. 'For you to try out. The newest products in our range.' She was welcomed everywhere, as she bought and bought to fill her cards as soon as possible.

'Isn't she growing!' (to my mother about me)

'I expect she's too big for a sweetie now?' (to my mother about me)

'How lucky she came out unscathed.' (the pharmacist in a whisper to my mother when she went to collect her supply of tranquillisers; on prescription, of course, always on prescription and always from the same doctor, as that doctor knew how difficult things were for my mother 'the grief-stricken widow'; and he also knew how she was devoting herself day and night to her daughter, the semi-orphan)

'Say thank you, Odette. Did you say thank you? I didn't hear. If you mumble people can't hear you.'

The pharmacist had a sweet for me too, or an Easter egg, and said I was getting such a big girl. My mother was very lucky to have such a strapping daughter. It was lovely to see mother and daughter together, inseparable.

Once after much pestering she had allowed me to go to a sports camp with my cousin. My aunt had rung her and told her she was making herself ridiculous by forbidding me to go.' 'Are you going to tie her to you all your life?' she had asked. My mother had been furious with her sister. Where the hell did her sister get the idea that she was tying me to her? Did she tie me to her when I went to school? Did she tie me to her when I went skating, with my cousin at that? That proved her sister was acting in bad faith. No one was in a better position than my aunt to know that my mother allowed me plenty of freedom. If she had her doubts about that camp, it was out of concern for me. Could I cope with being away from home for so long? She knew me better than I knew myself. She knew how I was inclined to overestimate myself. 'You need me, Odette. Go to that camp and we'll see which of the two of us misses the other first—and the most.' She put her signature on the enrolment form, which apart from that was completely filled out, wrote a cheque, slipped them both into an envelope, stuck a stamp on it and—without me—went to post the letter. I ran after her. I was suddenly terrified that she would throw herself under a car. She pretended not to see me. I couldn't go back home, as I didn't have a latchkey. I followed her like a little dog. She ignored me. But I saw her put the letter in the post box. And I was happy, so happy.

Two weeks before I was due to leave, she started pulling her hair out. Literally. She showed me the tufts. She maintained it was falling out, but it wasn't. She was pulling it out. She called me the most ungrateful child in the world. How could I leave her all alone for ten days? Was that what she'd sacrificed herself for me for, day and night? I acted as if I was deaf. I put aside the things I was going to take and phoned my cousin every day. Her father, my uncle, was to take us to the camp and they would provide an extra sheet sleeping bag for me, as I didn't have one and didn't know how or where to buy one. I was determined not to give in. The night before the camp my mother cried so bitterly, *and* she used my father's last handkerchief to wipe away her tears. That handkerchief lay on the cabinet in front of his photo. She had never used it before. It was as if she was saying: look, I'm already dead. I'm drying my tears with the handkerchief of death. I couldn't leave her alone. I was frightened she would hang or gas herself. I did not want to come home to an empty house, or to a house where my mother was dangling from the chandelier or lying in the bath with her wrists slashed. She had said so often that she wanted to be with my father. She stayed alive for me. I didn't want to drive her to her death.

First she flung her arms round me, but less than an hour later she started blaming me for throwing money down the drain. I must learn to be consistent. That was when I was afraid I was going mad. She was driving me mad. In order to be free of her nagging I paid back the enrolment fee out of my savings. She tore up the notes in front of me. Halfway through the camp she decided she wanted to visit my cousin, and I had to go with her. That really was the last straw. I took a Valium of hers, as I was afraid I wouldn't be able to control myself if she told people there that we were inseparable. So inseparable that I had decided to stay with her at the last minute, since 'Odette can't do without me.'

On the way home she said that my cousin was starting to look common. 'Did you see her cleavage? If you ask me that camp is a pretext for hooking a man. Sport doesn't interest her!' Behind her back I popped a second Valium in my mouth. My cousin had refused to say a word to me. She wouldn't even look at me. From that day on I regularly stole pills from my mother. She must have known. There's no way she didn't notice.

In the past, says Anouk, all inmates were given sedatives, often without their knowing it. The pills were crushed and mixed in with their food. That doesn't happen anymore. Prisoners' rights are respected.

'What about camphor?' asked someone, trying to be clever. Someone trying to ingratiate themselves with Anouk. But we all want to do that here.

Anouk was not looking at her, but at me. 'Why are you smiling?' she asked.

'Sorry,' I stammered, and covered my mouth with my hand.

'You can smile,' she said. 'It's not forbidden to smile.' To prove her point, she smiled, revealing her crooked teeth. 'Would you like to tell us why you were smiling?'

I shook my head and looked at the floor. After a while I dared to look up again. Again Anouk's eyes shot in my direction. I smiled feebly. She nodded in approval.

Later she called me over to her. 'Did he not allow you to smile?' she asked.

'No,' I said.

'You're beautiful when you smile, Odette. You should show us your smile more often.'

Thank God no one could hear her.

Sometimes he allowed me to smile, sometimes not. Some days I wasn't allowed to do anything. Then I would hold my breath. Literally.

I could keep it up for ages.

And the children had to hold their breath too. If they didn't do it of their own accord, I helped them with a pill from M's cupboard. The dogs were given one too. Everything and everyone kept quiet. But sometimes it still wasn't quiet enough.

If there was no Xanax, I gave them Lexotan or Temesta, or Valium. But the Valium was for M. I didn't like it: Valium reminded me of my mother.

According to Anouk all women in prison have a poor self-image.

'That's where it begins,' she says. 'With one's self-image.'

And she shows photos of how she used to look. 'I didn't like myself,' she said. 'I didn't believe I could be beautiful. Beauty starts here.'

She places the tips of the fingers of her right hand between her breasts. She glances at them. Then she looks at me, and she smiles.

Anouk organises workshops to boost our self-image. If you want to be on good terms with Anouk you must take part in those workshops. Everyone wants to be on good terms with Anouk, because she writes reports on us. We sit in a circle and have to say in turn how we see ourselves. Then we have to choose someone and say nice things about her.

I am never chosen. So Anouk says things about me, about my hair, for instance, or my eyes, but mostly about my hair. Afterwards they all make fun of me. Or they pull my hair. The last time when I got back to my cell there was a pair of scissors lying there. I sat for a long time holding those scissors. I even cut a piece of my hair off. My golden angel's hair, as Anouk calls it. I didn't mention the scissors to her.

When I was first here they gave me Xanax. They asked me if I wanted anything and I said: Xanax.

Anouk said: 'You don't need that Xanax.'

Then I realised it was a test. I had to prove that I could manage without Xanax. For the first few weeks I was tossing and turning all night. The beds are so narrow here! And the mattress isn't hard enough. I daren't say anything about it, but I had back ache day and night. We had such a good bed. M had bought it cheaply, together with a spacious wardrobe and two bedside tables, one for him and one for me. He drove round a lot in his van and whenever he saw a special offer or a sale, he always checked to see if there was anything for us among the items. Usually he waited until the final day or even the final hour of the final day before returning. Sometimes they gave things away for almost nothing. 'You must never pay the full whack,' he said. That whole bedroom suite cost us fifteen thousand francs. Mattresses included, how about that? They even threw in two lamps for the bedside tables. The price tags were still on them when he brought them home. Six hundred and forty-nine francs. Each! Who pays that much for a stupid lamp?

Of course the bed stayed at his place. After the move I never slept in it again. But I did go and lie in it a few times with the children when M was back in prison yet again and I had to look after his house. I was so tired, then, so, so tired. Since Elise's birth I had never slept for more than two hours at a stretch. I said to Gilles: 'If you're a good boy, we'll all go and lie in Daddy's big bed!' As if it was a reward. Within five minutes he was fed up with it. 'But we lived here, you, Jérôme, Daddy and me. You often came in to see us in the mornings. Jérôme's cot was next to our bed. You played here a lot. Perhaps we'll come back and live here again one day.' Whatever I said, he always wanted to get away as soon as possible. Eventually I simply made sure that everything was in order. I got the post, locked the door and left.

If W had still been alive, I could have asked him to move M's bed to the farmhouse and mine to M's house. If we put them back again just before he got out and if everyone kept their mouth shut, M need never know.

But W was no longer alive. M had already got rid of him. Like in gangster films.

Whenever I couldn't sleep in my cell, I imagined I was in my bed, not in M's house, but in the farmhouse, where I lived for two years with the children. In my mind I sat up. I looked into Elise's cot, got out of bed very carefully and went to the door on tiptoe. Usually I wore an old white T-shirt and panties. I opened the door gently. I stood listening in the hall to see if everything was in order. Sometimes I could hear Gilles snoring. He and Jérôme slept in the room next to mine. Boys with boys, girls with girls. Once I had satisfied myself that all was quiet, I crept to the kitchen. I carefully opened the door of the medicine cabinet and blindly grabbed the dose of Xanax. If I repeated that a few times in my mind, I became calmer, as if I had actually taken a Xanax, and as if the children were actually with me.

Jérôme was a light sleeper. He woke up at the slightest sound. Gilles sometimes screamed in his sleep, without waking up. When I heard it I jumped out of bed and rushed to their room. Jérôme would be sitting with his hands over his ears, next to or even under his bed. And Gilles went on screaming, while I tried to calm him down. 'Shush now, quiet, it's a nightmare, you're here with Mummy and Jérôme and Elise. Sometimes I had to shake him awake because he went on screaming. The tears poured down his cheeks. He clung to me sobbing. That child had been through too much too young. If it was very bad, I let him sleep in my bed with me. And I had the greatest difficulty in keeping Jérôme in his bed. I left both bedroom doors ajar, so that Jérôme could come to me if there was anything wrong and I was sure to hear him. But if I didn't hear anything, I was still worried. In M's childhood home all the children slept together in one room. There were two bedrooms, one for the parents and one for the children. One night M couldn't hear one of his brothers, although the brother always made noises in his sleep. At first M didn't dare turn the light on, as his parents had forbidden it, but fortunately he did it anyway. The boy was no longer breathing! M went and woke his parents, although that was strictly forbidden too. His father had to give his brother mouth-to-mouth resuscitation and he was saved. When I thought of that I took Jérôme into my bed too. And I assured the boys that they could always call me if there was something wrong. And they could also turn on the light. Jérôme could already do that. There was a string attached to the switch, and when he pulled on it the light went on and off. He knew it wasn't a toy. He was such a bright little chap. And a sweetie! He's like my Daddy, I often thought. A heart of gold.

He's still the most loving of the three. The one who visits me most often and always tries to bring a present. The drawings he has done for me! I have kept them all, in a folder. With his name on it. Jérôme. Sweet, gentle Jérôme. Too gentle, I sometimes fear.

So there we were, the three of us in one bed, and Elise next to us in her cot. 'It's all right just this once,' I said, 'but you're getting too big to sleep with your Mummy.' I didn't want to repeat my mother's mistakes and bring the children into my bed because otherwise I would be alone. I had sworn that during my first pregnancy: I'm not going to become a mother like my mother. Not like Mummy.

I won't say a bad word about her. She did her best for me. In her way she did her best. And I should be grateful to her for not bringing a stepfather into the house who might have abused me. 'I'm not letting the cat get at the cream,' she said. But she didn't always make things easy for me. My God!

Children must be able to go their own way, says Anouk, say I, says everyone.

I could have asked a warder for a sleeping pill, but that would have been immediately passed on to Anouk. I wanted to prove to Anouk that I didn't need any pills. And I don't need them.

'You see that you're strong,' she said.

Was it a trap? Should I have proved that I was weak and so completely helpless in the clutches of that monster M? Should I have demonstrated how he had made me into a completely dependent pill junkie?

The questions they dare to ask me here! Whether it's true he had a big penis. Whether it's true he had a small penis. Whether it's true he had a crooked penis. That he had three penises. Could do it seven times running. Could do it ten times running. Had lost his virginity to an older man. Had lost his virginity to an older woman. Had been a prostitute. Hated gays because he was gay himself, a closet gay. Masturbated in his sleep. Always used a condom when he raped a woman. Never used a condom when he raped a woman. Was scared of AIDS, wasn't scared of AIDS. Wanted sex with young girls because they didn't have sexually transmitted diseases. Was too mean to buy porn and so made his own. Forced me to film him when he had sex with other women. Forced me to have sex with the dogs. Taught the dogs to have sex with me. Never washed his penis. Washed his penis three times a day. Had big balls. Small balls. Only one ball. Hair on his scrotum. No hair on his scrotum. Tumour on one ball. Circumcised. Uncircumcised. Wart on scrotum. Tight foreskin. Loose foreskin. Lots of sperm. Not much sperm. White sperm. Translucent sperm. Salty sperm.

And whether it's true what his father said about him: that he and his brother were jealous of the prick of a third brother, and that they pulled for all they were worth to make their pricks longer.

That family would do better to keep their mouths shut.

M pulled his prick a lot, not to make it longer, but to harden it like steel.

It wasn't him I had to obey, but his penis. And he had to obey it too. If you don't understand that, you can't understand M, or me.

His penis wasn't big, but neither was Napoleon's.

And like Napoleon he wore a hat, which he sometimes took off, to greet someone, or to leap into action.

'Do you miss it?' they hissed in my ear. And they rub their hands over their breasts, or grab their cunts. They stand there as though they need to piss. As long as they keep their hands off me, they can do what they like. I can't hear it and I can't see it. But I know what I think about it. The great danger in a prison is that you forget your manners, abandon them, lose the knack—that you descend to their level.

Some women in here could do with a stiff dose of camphor every day.

In the army they used to put camphor in the coffee. My mother told me that my father told her that. Otherwise those young men would be far too horny. When my father was due for leave and was going to see my mother, he didn't drink a drop of that coffee. 'He didn't want to disappoint me,' said my mother coyly. The coffee in that army was so weak that you could see Napoleon riding through it on his horse, and you could smell the camphor.

That was why I had to smile when Anouk talked about camphor. I saw Napoleon riding his white horse through a ditch of weak coffee, with his hand tucked under the panel of his coat. And with his hat, of course.

Every summer my mother and I went to see the Battle of Waterloo. It was performed on the battlefield in June by amateur actors. The people who took part practised throughout the year. It had to be accurate down to the smallest details.

If I get out I'd like to go again, with the children. Gilles has been a couple of times, but the two youngest haven't. They will love it.

'War was completely different then from what it is

now,' said my mother, taking Daddy's binoculars out of her bag. 'Here, you have a look too. Can you see Napoleon?'

Napoleon rode the largest and whitest horse. Even without binoculars you had to be blind to miss him.

That would have been something for M, dressed as Napoleon, surveying and leading his troops. And driving them to their death in hordes.

5

That young guy who murdered those babies in that day nursery acts as if he's insane. Soon he'll have to face a jury but if he can convince the investigators that he's insane, he won't be put on trial. He'll simply be sent detained at the discretion of the court.

Well, simply. It seems it's worse than ordinary detention. Some people never get out, except in a box. It's not easy to get the 'not of sound mind' classification. You need an expert lawyer, or a solid dossier. It is even more difficult to be subsequently reclassified as responsible for one's actions.

At first they were going to sentence me to indefinite detention. Not now, but long ago, almost twenty-five years ago. I didn't have a clue in those days. The court's psychiatrist had studied my case and concluded that I was not myself. I wasn't responsible for my actions; otherwise I wouldn't have done those things. She had made inquiries and had heard everywhere how exemplary my behaviour had been. A dutiful daughter and mother, who looked after her son well and studied the Bible. At that time I went to meetings of the Jehovah's

Witnesses every Tuesday with M's first wife and her new husband, the man she had picked up at that party where M acted as DJ. Because I was a single mother, I didn't have to go from door to door recruiting. M wouldn't have wanted me to do that. He was radically opposed to everything to do with religion. Like his father, who said to his children: 'You don't need a god. God the Father is me!' With that blasphemy he brought down doom on the heads of his children. But they hadn't learned their lesson, because when M had children of his own, he thought: now it's my turn to play God the Father.

Pride comes before a fall. Ask Lucifer. Ask M.

M was on remand in prison and couldn't forbid me to go to the Bible meetings. I didn't say a word about it to him. But I did to Mummy, who discovered the Bible together with me, and who regretted not having sent me to a Christian school. That had been a mistake, but fortunately it was being made up for now. Later M made fun of Mummy and me about it, but we were above his scornful laughter, like the first Christians. Unfortunately we could not stop him burning all my Bibles, including the one I had been given by his first wife, in which she had written the names of all his children. He poured petrol over them and set light to them with a match.

In hell devils will pour petrol over him and throw a match in the pool of petrol. Or they will crown him Devil-in-Chief.

The court's psychiatrist said that I was under tremendous pressure. I did not have the mental strength to resist the constant humiliations and manipulation. I had been brainwashed *and* I was taking the wrong medication. I needed help, she concluded. I looked for it in the Bible, but I needed medical help. If I were detained indefinitely, I would get it.

It was all in my file.

M disagreed. He had time to get to the bottom of things. If he couldn't find what he wanted in the prison library, he asked for information through his lawyer. He came to the conclusion that I would be acquitted at appeal, and so he forced me to launch one. The upshot was that I was given five years instead of three. And I wasn't detained at the discretion of the court. I wasn't given any treatment, although I was in urgent need of it.

It was always the same with M. If he had read an article about something, he thought he was cleverer than people who had studied the subject for years.

Thank God *Dieu merci* I was released after two years, less than two years actually. They could also see that I didn't belong in a prison. And they felt guilty about that miscarriage when I was on remand. They owed me something. I had a young son. A mother must be at home with her son, or he will come to a sticky end.

This time I did take Xanax. There was no Anouk there, for whom I had to give it up. Nor was there a Sister Virginie, visiting me. There was the stream of letters from M, with instructions. So many letters! Sometimes two a day, in that small handwriting of his. I could scarcely decipher them. But I read them all, and I answered, not every letter, but often. At the time I wrote most to my mother, as she was looking after Gilles. Someone had to look after him. I wrote letter after letter in which I poured my heart out. My feelings emptied themselves onto the paper. I begged her to say to Gilles that I loved him very much and thought of him at every moment of the day and night, and would she give him lots of kisses from his Mummy and give me kisses too in her mind, as I missed her, she was my darling Mummy, if she abandoned me I would die. 'Please be sure to hold his hand tight in the street, Mummy, because he'll pull himself loose if something catches his attention. It may be a bird, a cyclist, or a pebble. He's stronger than you think, Mummy—and faster.' And would she not give him too many sweets, as sugar made him agitated. And he shouldn't watch more than one hour's television a day, preferably not violent programmes, as they made him excited. And would she stand over him when he cleaned his teeth, since otherwise he didn't brush them properly. I put cards for Gilles in the envelope with a drawing on them. Or I cut something out for him that I had seen in a magazine, a horse or a chicken, or a tractor. My mother had told him that I had been admitted to a clinic and had to stay there till I was better. And his Daddy was sick too, but he was in a different clinic. What are you supposed to tell a child like that?

There was a mother-and-child section in that prison for children up to three. Gilles was already five. That was a pity, since otherwise I would have been able to keep him with me, but when he came to visit me he was able to play with the other children in the play area. Those mothers were given cooking and knitting classes and lessons on nutrition and child care, and that's how I learned to knit. I started with a scarf but by the end I could knit sweaters. The last thing I knitted for Gilles was a red sweater with the head of Mickey Mouse on it. My mother had chosen the wool with him. He wore the jersey for ages, and he was proud of it. He told everyone who would listen that his Mummy had knitted it for him in the clinic.

My mother said: ‘I never wanted to send you to a nuns’ school because they make the girls there crochet and knit from morning till night, and now you’re learning it in here!’

I think she was jealous. I could knit and she couldn’t. I think that’s sad, and petty-minded.

The day nursery murderer maintains he heard voices, voices that instructed him to force his way into the day nursery and stab as many people, grown-ups and babies, as possible. The blood must splash over the walls and the toys and the beds and sheets. The more blood the better. But those voices didn’t put a revolver to his head. They didn’t threaten to pull the trigger if he didn’t do what they told him. I know I mustn’t hide behind excuses. There are no excuses for what I’ve done. That first prison sentence of two years, plus two months on remand, was well-deserved. ‘You were at the wheel of the van when M was hunting for girls, Odette. You could have driven to a police station. You could have accelerated instead of braking. Those are the choices you made, or didn’t make.’

Yes, Anouk. Of course, Anouk.

If she is absolutely certain that I was at the wheel of the van, then I was at the wheel of the van. If she says I could have reported it to the police, then I could have reported it to the police. And of course I shouldn’t have married him. He was in prison at the time and I wasn’t, yet. I had no reason at all to be frightened of him. He couldn’t do anything to me. Why did I marry him? I was no longer the naïve, infatuated girl. I knew what he was capable of. It was his fault that I had been on remand and had had a miscarriage. There was a trial hanging over my head. I could be detained indefinitely or go to jail. What illusions did I still have?

That is all true, but I also knew that they weren't going to keep him in prison forever. Sooner or later he would be released and I would have to pay the price for everything I had done wrong in his eyes. I had no choice. He would take his revenge. I knew what he was capable of. I wanted to shelter and keep sheltering under the umbrella of his protection. For as long as he needed me, he wouldn't dispose of me. I had to convince him he could count on me and that I would obey him blindly. And that he needed me. He rang me from prison every day, and he sent letters with instructions. Getting married would make a good impression on the court, he said, both in his case and in mine. We had to get married.

They should have forbidden him to ring me. But no, he got brownie points for ringing me. It proved that he cared about his family. Day and night I heard his voice in my head. Do this, do that. Be quiet. Speak. Buy this, sell that. Why didn't they forbid him to ring me? They encouraged him! I went to the Jehovah's Witnesses Bible meetings in the hope of finding God. If He protected me I could break with M. But I was frightened it would leak out. My fear was greater than my faith. I didn't find God then because I thought more about M than about God. He was my god. 'No man can serve two masters, for he will hate the one and love the other.' Matthew 6:24. I didn't hate God, but I couldn't love him. There wasn't enough room for Him in my head and my heart. I was like the Israelites who worshipped the golden calf. God spoke thus to Moses: 'thy people have corrupted themselves... now let me alone that my wrath may wax hot against them, and that I may consume them.' Moses begged God to give his people a second chance. And God gave them a second chance. But when Moses saw the golden calf, he himself was so angry that he smashed the stone tablets on the ground.

I too worshipped a god. And I was given a second chance, which I squandered. I regret it from the bottom of my heart. I am so sorry.

Give me a third chance, God. Please.

I ask You on my knees and with both my hands folded.

In fairy tales everyone gets three chances. A man and a woman were granted three wishes because they had saved someone's life. The woman said: I'd like a juicy sausage, and immediately she had a sausage in her hand. The man said: you hare brain, I wish that sausage were hanging from your nose. And then they had to use the third wish to get the sausage off her nose again.

My Daddy told me that story. And he drew a woman with a big sausage on the tip of her nose. The sausage pointed upwards in an arc. 'What would you use your three wishes for, Odette? A wish for Daddy, a wish for Mummy and one for yourself? Yes! Come to Daddy. Give your Daddy a kiss.'

And I gave him a kiss. I couldn't think of any wishes. Back then I had everything I could wish for.

Wish number one: let me forget everything he ever said. Wipe it from my memory.

Wish number two: ensure my children are safe and healthy, and never fall in love with a devil or a she-devil.

Wish number three: give me a third chance. Please.

There is nothing grimmer than getting married in prison. There was no reception, no beautiful white dress, there were no bridesmaids, no presents, no family. There was a document to which we and our witnesses had to put our signatures. My mother didn't want to come. That worked out well, as I didn't want her to come. At the same time I thought it was dreadful that she wasn't there. She wouldn't let me invite my aunt. She didn't want the family to know. It wasn't a wedding, she said, but a farce. It should be forbidden by law to marry a criminal. My mother forgot that I had in the meantime been on remand myself.

Mummy and I had talked so often about the dinner service she was going to give me when I got married, and about the caterer she would engage, and about the dress, which would also be her own dress in some small part, since she had got married in a tailored suit. My parents had married a year after the war. 'That's why I wore a suit,' said my mother. 'And your father wore his army uniform, as his suits were worn out, or maybe he had none. But there was a reception, sober, yes, like everything at the time, but still a party.' My father's friends formed a guard of honour for the young couple. They also wore their army uniforms and raised their sabres proudly. The very same day my parents left for their honeymoon in Spa, the town where Marie Henriette, second queen of the Belgians, had sought refuge while her husband, Leopold II, was living in Brussels in the palace with a girl young enough to be his grandchild.

The whole family, my mother said, was depraved. With the exception of Marie Henriette, whose villa my parents had visited. And they had drunk from the same fountain from which the queen had quenched her thirst daily. That woman had borne her fate with great dignity. In Spa they were still always full of praise for her. And did I know how frivolously Marie Henriette's daughters had behaved?

I knew, because my mother had a book in which it was revealed in minute detail. She had bought it in Spa at the time. In the album of photos of their wedding and honeymoon there were photos in which first she and then my father posed with the book.

Like Marie Henriette my mother had never lived in sin. Both of them had tried in vain to set their daughters a good example. 'Somehow I must have had a premonition of how much she and I would turn out to have in common.' My father would have preferred to go to Bouillon. 'Something was pulling me towards Spa,' said my mother.

On his deathbed Leopold had wanted his relationship with that woman of easy virtue to be officially recognised. The Church had acceded to his wishes, but parliament refused. Such marriages made a mockery of the institution. They did not expunge the stain of licentiousness. They were a slap in the face of all those who were respectably married.

I had also pictured my wedding differently, but my mother didn't stop to consider that. She didn't even give me the diamond earrings which she had always promised I could have when I got married, the earrings she had been given by Daddy for their tenth anniversary. I did not have the courage to ask her for them.

Elise has them now. She wanted to give them to me. She said: 'Mummy, I'm too young for diamonds,' but I said: 'No, darling, they're for you. Keep them for later. One day you'll get married, to a good man. It's better that I have nothing. Everything I have will be taken away from me.'

'Is it true that you and Daddy got married in prison?' she asked.

I nodded and was deeply ashamed.

On M's side there was only his eldest brother, who acted as his witness. And M's first wife was my witness. M had rung her and told her she must be my witness. And she must give her wedding ring to me, the ring M had bought for her when he married *her.*

'It'll bring bad luck,' I said.

That look!

He demanded that I wear a ring, but did not want to buy a new ring for me. I wore that wedding ring for almost ten years. With her name and their wedding date engraved on it.

After the 'ceremony' we were entitled to two hours together in the 'bridal suite'. Our witnesses looked after Gilles, since we could scarcely say to him: sit on a chair here for two hours while Mummy and Daddy make love.

I was so nervous! And so was he. We hadn't had sex for almost three years. That's how long he had been inside. In a prison you have to be married to have sex. That is the law.

'There are lots of women I could be lying here with,' he said. And I had to thank him. He squeezed my nipples hard. 'Thank you,' I said. He squeezed harder.

I was still his.

I remember everything he said.

Patience, Odette. Says Anouk, says Sister Virginie, says everyone.

I've been patient for so long.

He didn't want our children to go to a day nursery. No babysitters were allowed to come. 'We're not in the Congo here.' There it was normal to employ a nanny, but here it was unnatural. And even in the Congo strict rules had to be observed. His mother had made it clear to the nanny from the outset that she was there for the bottles and the nappies and the bath, not for cuddles and kisses. The staff had to know their place, especially in a country like the Congo, which still had a long way to go in its development. The boys and *boyesses* came straight from the bush into a civilised environment. Often they didn't know where the limits were. At the beginning they behaved shyly, but if you loosened the reins for a moment, their bashfulness turned to impudence in less than no time. Before you realised they brought half their family over to camp in the garden. They built a hut, lit a fire and sat quietly cooking, as if they had always lived there. 'Everyone is related to everyone else there.'

But the main fear was that the nanny would one day disappear with the baby. Witch doctors were on the lookout for white babies for their potions and powders. Every part of such babies was used, even the downy hairs on their backs. Baby's testicles were especially prized, and the foreskin of the penis. Once when his parents came home from the club, his mother had seen the nanny through the window bending over the baby and muttering. She's putting a spell on him! she had thought in a panic and had rushed indoors to snatch him out of her arms. Although it was a sultry tropical night, she had felt icy cold, and also guilty for having left him with that Negress. She had resolved to go out less. Or if she did go out she would take him with her.

There's nowhere better for a child to be than with his mother.

Unless that mother is called Geneviève Lhermitte.

His father hadn't forgotten the nanny either after all those years. 'Such a beautiful kid,' he said, 'with such slender arms and legs. Like a gazelle.' One afternoon he taught her to play chess. The baby was sleeping peacefully, the boys were at work in the kitchen and in the yard behind the house, and his wife was having coffee with friends somewhere. He had had a chessboard made of ebony and ivory. At first he just wanted to let her admire the craftsmanship with which each piece had been sculpted, but very soon he could not ignore her desire to learn. Patiently he had taught her the names: king, rook, queen, pawn, bishop, and then the various moves. She had picked it up very quickly. After that they wasted no opportunity to practise, whenever they had the place to themselves. Now and then he deliberately created an opening for her. He never needed to point it out. She always pounced at once, like a leopard, or a hunter. She never laughed during the game, not even when he let her win, which he did not do often, in order not to awaken her suspicion. 'Other men would have taken advantage of the situation, but not me. She knew she was safe with me. A woman is never as beautiful as when she feels at ease. Then she relaxes and shows herself as she really is. That was enough for me. I was happy being able to look at those carbuncle eyes and that black gleaming skin. I would have taken her along to the chess club, but it was for whites only. It was too good to last. Jealous eyes had spied on us and Desiderata had to leave. I still wonder what became of her. She could have become a really good chess player, a grandmistress.' And he said that he had always expected M to go looking for black velvet or.... 'What they've known as babies...'

'A chess-playing black babe,' said M, winking at me. 'My father studied psychology.'

'We did psychology, yes,' said his father. 'It was an important subject. I never had problems with the staff, or with my pupils. With my colleagues, yes, but not with the children in my class. And that was because I knew how to treat them. Rule number one: make it clear who's boss.'

'And were you the boss, Dad?'

'Of course. There are only two possibilities: either you are the boss and are respected, or you're not the boss and they walk all over you. A real boss can't afford to slacken the reins. He draws the chalk lines that must not be crossed and ensures that they are not crossed. Even Desiderata wouldn't have dreamt of abusing the bond that slowly but surely grew between us. When I snapped my fingers, she knew that was the end of chess, even if there was no reason at all. There did not have to be a reason. It was enough that I snapped my fingers. And because I was the boss I had to snap my fingers now and then. She understood that and accepted it. And so I could behave mildly and magnanimously without her seeing it as weakness, a weakness she would inevitably have exploited. I could in a manner of speaking leave the door of her cage open. She wouldn't have abused it. I hope you're the boss, son.'

They both focused on me simultaneously.

'She's well trained,' said M. He took a nut from a dish and threw it in my direction. 'Catch!' he ordered, just as he would later call to the dogs. The nut bounced off my breast and fell to the floor.

'The nuts are a reward,' said his father. 'You only reward her with a nut when she has carried out an order properly. Say for example: get a glass of Coke for your husband and your father-in-law.'

'Did you hear what my father asked?'

'He didn't ask anything,' I stammered.

'Get two glasses of Coke, Odette. One for my father and one for me.'

I was rooted to the spot.

'Do as I say, Odette.'

I looked from the father to the son. They became one man, a two-headed monster. Looking back I often thought: that's when I should have left. If it was not just in him, but in the father too, then it was in his blood, in his pores, even in his hair. It would only get worse. It would teem, ferment and fester.

I didn't understand how the two of them could doubt their kinship.

'I'll count to three, Odette. One, two...'

I should have let him think that I was going to get the damned Coke and should have left the house by the back door never to return. But Gilles was having his afternoon nap upstairs in his bed. I couldn't possibly leave him behind with those two.

Like a robot I went to the kitchen. I pulled open the fridge, took out the bottle of Coke, filled two glasses and served them to the gentlemen. M threw a nut at me; I caught it with my hand and put it in my mouth.

'Needs a bit more practice,' said the father drily.

M had never thrown nuts before. Ever.

And the father probably set the son other bad examples.

He wouldn't have treated a Negress like a circus monkey. Oh no. The gent had been a colonial, but he was not a racist. He was a good colonial, 'because they existed, even if that is forgotten now.' He would have initiated her into the noble game of chess to prove how broad-minded he was.

If I had wanted, M would have taught me to play chess, but chess didn't interest me. Or M either. He had played chess with his father in the past because his father demanded it, and he was the only one in the family with the brains for it, but he preferred to put his energy into other things.

As if someone had given a sign father and son raised the glasses of Coke to their lips. They emptied it in one greedy gulp, smacked their lips, wiped their mouths with the back of their hands and put the glasses down. Then they burped, and declared that it had hit the spot.

They deserved a nut for synchronised boorishness.

Catch!

'Odette,' M's father said pompously. 'M told me about your father. My deepest condolences.'

It was a very long time since anyone had offered me their condolences. It was also strange to be offered condolences for a father who had been dead for twenty years.

People usually said they were sorry.

I was sorry too.

He calls himself a father, I thought scornfully. How could the same word apply to him and my father?

Before he or M had the chance to ask me to refill their glasses, I lied that Gilles was awake. I couldn't stay another second in the same room as those two.

In the bathroom I filled the washbasin with cold water. I wanted to take something to calm me down, but the medicine cabinet was locked and the key was in M's trouser pocket. I plunged my hands in the water. I had learned that from my mother. 'My blood is boiling,' she complained, and said that she would have most liked to open her veins to be rid of that hot blood. She took a razor of my father's and ran it over the inside of her arms. 'What quality! After all those years, as sharp as ever.' My father had shaved morning and evening to please my mother. She liked a man with clean-shaven cheeks. Most of all she liked a man who did as he was told.

'Put it down, Mummy. Daddy wouldn't like you to cut yourself.'

'Daddy wouldn't like you to cut yourself,' she repeated mockingly. But she put it down.

One day she'll do it, I thought. Perhaps even in front of me.

When I was at home, I had to soak two face flannels in the cold water for her. I wrung them out gently and put one on her forehead and one on her neck. I stood beside her like that until she began to shake her head. Then I knew it was time to wet the flannels again. I turned on the tap and ran extra cold water into the washbasin. It always surprised me how quickly it warmed up. My mother's hands were heaters with a temperature of 37 degrees each. Her forehead and neck were also heaters, which I had to try to cool down with those two stupid face flannels. Sometimes she pushed me away roughly and submerged her head. Gasping for air she raised her head out of the water, and plunged it straight back in. She repeated this ritual three or four times. And she had me fetch buckets filled with cold water. She kicked off her shoes, took off her stockings and put one foot in each bucket. 'That's good. Oh, that's good!'

One afternoon she kept submerging her head, as if she was turning into a fish and could only breathe underwater. I turned on the cold water tap of the bath, ran downstairs and came back with ice cubes. I tipped them in with the cold water splashing into the bath.

'What are you up to?' she cried shrilly. 'Don't you dare push me in!'

For days afterwards she kept a strict watch on me. I wasn't allowed to pour coffee for her anymore, and I wasn't allowed to help her cook, because 'God knows what I would put into her food or drink.' She maintained that I knew that she could have died of a heart attack in the icy water. 'That's what you were hoping. Go on, admit it. I wasn't born yesterday, Odette.' She appealed to my father even more often than she usually did: 'Gilbert, Gilbert, why did you abandon me?' Gradually I began to believe her. I was a bad daughter and I was capable of luring my poor mother into a trap. Any murderess worth her salt looks her victim straight in the eye, but I had used a cowardly trick. I didn't contradict her when she called me evil. I nodded, and apologised. I was sorry. I was truly sorry. How could I have treated her so heartlessly? 'I've no one left now!' she wailed. She banished me from her bedroom. Instead of feeling liberated I stood outside her closed bedroom door begging to be let in. I was terrified that something would happen to her and that I would not be there to save her. I begged her to let me sleep with her, although I disliked doing so. My mother's snoring had often kept me awake, but now I pricked up my ears in the hope of hearing the familiar grunting sounds. While she suspected me of wanting to murder her, I could not get to sleep for fear that she would die. Then I would be an orphan. I had no brothers or sisters, only a dog, but Fifi was ancient and actually needed an injection. It wasn't the moment to bring that up. 'Does Fifi have to go too?' she would say.

Dogs were lucky. They could go to a sanctuary when they were rejected and kicked out. Where was I to go?

One night she was standing by my bed. I had finally fallen asleep and suddenly she was standing there in her long white nightdress. Just like a ghost.

She was trying to open up her arms with her sharp nails.

'Don't do that, Mummy.'

'It's got to come out!'

'No, no, you need your blood.'

'*Je souffre.*' How could I sleep while she suffered? She pouted like a girl of eight or ten.

She could have gone to the bathroom, but she had come to me. She needed me again.

Mummy, I thought with a sigh. How lucky that I hadn't invited her to the meal with M's father. *And* that I had not told M that I had been secretly fantasising about a possible friendship between his father and my mother. More than friendship even.

Imagine!

Breathe out, I thought. I mustn't forget to breathe out.

Breathing out is more important than breathing in. No one forgets to breathe in, but people sometimes forget to breathe out.

I breathed out as deeply as possible. With short puffs I expelled the last oxygen from my lungs. Puff, puff, puff.

My heart began beating more calmly. I closed my eyes and breathed out, out, out. The coolness of the water crept along my hands, wrists and arms. Whatever happened, I had to keep my head cool, and my blood and my heart. I must stay cool from top to toe. If we moved, I wanted to go and live in a house with a cool cellar. I would sit in it when the blood in my veins started surging. And in that marvellous coolness...

The bathroom door opened. M's father filled the doorway. His face looked even redder than just now, and he was panting. I hadn't heard him come upstairs. He must have crept up like a thief in the night.

'No need to be afraid,' he said, seeking for support with one hand. His ribcage was moving up and down fast. He was gasping for breath.

Out, out, out, I thought.

'I won't do anything to you.' He looked like actors in films just before they have a fatal heart attack. 'M told me I must leave you alone. I don't want to insult you, but you're not my type.'

He staggered into the bathroom and shut the door behind him. I stood staring at him with my hands in the water.

'I want to tell you something in private.'

'Where is he?'

'Downstairs.'

'What did you say to him?'

'That I needed a pee.'

'There's a toilet downstairs.

'That I couldn't find.'

I briskly pulled the plug out of the washbasin and dried my hands.

'There's something I think you should know, Odette. About my son, my eldest son. I never told his first wife, and I still regret it. Perhaps they would still be together if I had warned her. But then you and I wouldn't be standing talking to each other.'

'I know everything about him. He has no secrets from me.'

'And do you have any from him?'

I didn't answer. What business was it of his?

'You're very much in love, aren't you?'

I said nothing.

'Even when you're furious, you can't hide it. You can't hide anything. You'll learn.' He laughed and bared his ugly teeth.

I still said nothing.

'You're not the first one to fall in love with him and you won't be the last. But I hope you'll stay with him. My wife left me. That's the worst thing that can happen to a man. I was afraid I'd go mad. I did go mad, and needed treatment. I was as helpless as a baby. Have you ever been crazy, so crazy you had to be locked up?'

He gave me a penetrating look. Ugly nose, I thought. Nostrils you can look up into. Flabby chin. Hair as greasy and dishevelled as his son's.

'I have to go downstairs to get the food ready. If you've something to say to me, do it when M is there.'

He grabbed my wrists. 'Promise me you'll never leave him. Spare him that insult, and that pain.'

'Let me go!'

'I'll let you go when you listen to what I've got to say to you. Are you going to listen?'

Against my will I nodded. He let me go.

'You hurt me.'

'And you are making a fuss. I'll overlook it this once, but I don't like women who make a fuss. It's a sign of weakness and I like strong women—and strong men.' He clenched his fist to add force to his words. 'I've always set my children a good example. Without hesitation, the day I knew I was going to be a father I immediately gave up both alcohol and cigarettes. Overnight. I had no problem with that because I was motivated. A father can't afford to set a bad example. The children came first for me, always. When my wife and I met, we decided almost immediately that we wanted a big family. And we had lots of children. I don't know if they're all mine, but that's another matter. I brought them up as if they were my children. That's what counts. I made no distinction between those I was sure about and the others. A child is a child. As a parent you want the best for your child, but you can't control everything. You have to send them to school, they come into contact with local children, who may be less well brought-up. They pick up snatches of news reports, arguments and debates. They may get to see magazines that are not intended for their eyes. Sometimes you do something wrong without knowing it. You think you're doing the right thing, but it goes wrong. For example, I've always wondered whether we gave M a Cain complex.' Have you heard of the Cain complex?'

I shook my head.

'You know who Cain is?'

'He murdered his brother Abel.'

'Out of jealousy.'

'M has no problems with his brothers, or with his sister.'

'He won't admit it, but I know better. He was the only child. Suddenly he had to deal with a rival. I thought immediately: this is going to go wrong. We were in the Congo at the time, and I didn't have my textbooks with me. Back in Belgium I looked it up. There it was in black and white. Cain complex: unhealthy, destructive competition between brothers resulting in hatred and possibly murder. M is like Cain. He always wants to be the best. And the greatest, the strongest, the brightest, the funniest. Even when he's not. For a long time he was slightly built. It hurt him. We never talked about it, but I knew what was going on inside him, and is still going on. Try not to outdo him. You went to teacher training college, he didn't. That doesn't make you cleverer, or mean you know more. But even if you are smarter, never let him see that. Don't humiliate him. Don't fan the flames.'

I turned the tap on, cooled my hands under the stream of water, and put them against my glowing cheeks. Thank God he didn't make any stupid remarks about it.

'Anything else?' I asked haughtily.

'Yes.' He turned the tap off firmly, and continued his argument imperturbably. 'His mother and I both practised two-person competitive sports. Both judo and chess are a one-to-one battle, man against man, woman against woman. Or man against woman. One wins, the other loses. End of story. You look each other straight in the eye and have to eliminate each other. There is no alternative. You go on fighting until one of the two throws in the towel. That truth is rock hard, but also pure, honest. M imbibed that with his mother's milk.'

'That you have to eliminate each other?'

'Not literally. But his mother and I talked about it sometimes. Perhaps those conversations were not suitable for children's ears. I thought: a father has the duty to toughen up his sons. I mustn't spare them, I must teach them the basic rule, and that is the law of the jungle: I defeat him or he will defeat me. Win or lose. My father fought in the 1914-1918 war. He was a pilot in the Belgian air force. Next time I'll show you photos of him in the cockpit of his plane. A Spad. That means nothing to you, but it was a legendary machine, designed by the great Louis Blériot. Those planes had no ejector seat. They were flying soap boxes. Coffins. The rules were simple: you eliminated the enemy or the enemy eliminated you. That law applied on the ground too. The main thing was to be first to stick your bayonet in the enemy's belly. His belly or yours. I wanted to pass on that lesson to my children. They had to know the trials life would confront them with. Now I'm frightened that we have encouraged his assertiveness. I thought I had to make him assertive, but perhaps I should have toned it down. Don't make the same mistake as us. And don't challenge him. Don't enter into competition with him.'

'The army doesn't interest him. Nor do chess or judo. In his eyes it's all a waste of time.'

'For that very reason, Odette. For that very reason.'

He stepped aside. I could go, but now I wanted to know what he meant. At the same time I knew. The father meant that the son had no outlet for his need for competition. He and his wife had had one. And just as water finds a way through even the hardest stone, M's assertiveness would find a way out. The father dreaded to think what that might be.

'He did karate.'

'That was in the past, Odette.'

We looked each other in the eyes for a moment. Then he pulled the door open. 'You go first. He needn't know that we've talked.'

'He'll know. He always gets to know everything. Sooner or later.'

The thought flashed through my head that he was trying to impress me. Or to form an alliance with me behind M's back. It's not M but he who wants to be the strongest and the best. The father wants to outdo the son. Pathetic, I thought, and embarrassing.

M didn't have anything to prove. He *was* the strongest, and he knew it.

M had called it a typical *petite idée bourgeoise*, my wanting to invite his father. But he had phoned him. First he had called one of his brothers, who in turn had called another brother, who had called the sister and so had got hold of a number at which he should be able to reach his father. After trying three or four times he got him on the line, and father and son fixed a date. Father was looking forward eagerly to meeting the new wife *and* his new grandson. He could already walk, but by now the father was used to his children getting married and having children without telling him.

M did not interfere when I laid the table with the table linen I had been given by my mother and that she had actually wanted to give me as a wedding present, but it was a shame to leave it in the cupboard and in a certain sense, she had added magnanimously, I was married now. I repeated her words to M: that it was a shame to leave the table linen in the cupboard. After that afternoon it never wound up in the cupboard again. The napkins—embroidered personally by my grandmother—were used as rags, and the tablecloth itself served for years to cover an old motorbike. Sometimes I think I shall go to hell because I didn't take care of the table linen over which Granny bent for hours and hours, embroidering lilies-of-the-valley on it with the finest possible stitches.

But that morning I thought I would often lay the table festively for M's family or mine. I even bought flowers and put them in a vase on the table in the hall, as I had always seen my mother do when her parents came to visit. Or my father's parents, or her sister. And I cleaned the house and washed my hair and put a new blouse on.

M didn't make any sarcastic remarks. More than that, he followed my example, shaved, put on a clean shirt and announced he would take care of dessert. He went round the house whistling.

I thought: you see. He's missed his father all this time. He won't admit it, but now he's coming, he's as happy as a sand boy.

And I was happy too. Because yes, I was a *petite bourgeoise*. I *am* a *petite bourgeoise.*

M is not a hunter, but a poacher. The poacher puts out traps. The hunter doesn't. The brilliant poacher lets the animals put out the trap themselves.

M was a brilliant poacher. Sometimes.

On that day, that memorable Sunday on which his father was finally to meet his eldest son's new partner, and their little son, his actions approached genius. He didn't suggest that I cook steak and chips. He didn't have to. He knew that I would buy the most tender and juiciest beef steak. I had placed a knife with a serrated edge by each plate to cut the meat. And I had put the mayonnaise for the chips in a china dish on the table. And next time, I said to M, I'll ask my mother to give me her recipe for coq-au-vin.

Even then he did not say that his father hadn't eaten meat for years.

'How would you like your steak?' I asked him. 'M and I like it rare.'

At first I thought he had not heard my question. So I asked it again. The father did not say: didn't my son tell you I'm a vegetarian? The father sat down at table without a word. I served the meat rare for all three of us. He didn't touch it, just ate some chips.

'Isn't it cooked enough?' I asked.

'You can cook it whatever way you like. I don't eat meat.'

I went as red as the blood that had leaked out of the rare beefsteak.

'Odette always thinks that everyone lives like she and her mother,' said M. 'She has learned a lot, but she still has a long way to go.' He stuck his knife into his father's steak and swung it onto his own plate. The father dunked a chip in the mayonnaise and popped it in his mouth. I picked up my knife and gouged the beautiful white table linen. Three times I cut it. Then M took the knife away from me.

When he had gone I remembered the jar of peas in the cupboard. But I couldn't have served him peas and chips, could I? Even if I had known he was a vegetarian, I wouldn't have known what to make for him. What do vegetarians eat?

'He doesn't drink alcohol, he doesn't smoke, doesn't eat meat,' said M afterwards. 'But he does screw.' He pushed me against the wall. 'Did you see how he looked at you?' And he told me not to let him in if I was home alone, not to let anyone in if he wasn't there. 'A woman like you can't trust any man, not even men who say they want to be like a father to you. Especially not those.'

M's father had not said that. He had no paternal ambition with regard to me. On the contrary. I was to call him by his first name, he said, and Gilles was to do the same.

'He can't talk yet,' I had replied.

'My father is afraid that the girls won't want him anymore if they know he has grandchildren,' said M.

'I can assure you that Granddads do very well on the market.'

Father and son had burst out laughing. It was when they had recovered from the fit of laughter that the father had suggested an excursion to the family farmhouse, but M's mood had changed abruptly. He had announced brusquely that he had to go and look at a car, which might have an engine that still had some mileage in it.

M had smiled at his father. 'Do you see what I mean? In her world and in her head people don't work on Sundays. People visit each other. They eat cake, drink coffee, gossip and chat.'

'I wouldn't mind having a look at that engine,' said the father. 'Is it a diesel?'

M nodded. 'Six cylinder. Renault.'

'Do you remember that oil pit I'd dug in our garage and cased in concrete? It was a nice, professional pit. You always stood and watched when I was working on the car. I remember the first time that you handed me the right spanner without my asking for it. I thought: he'll go a long way. You didn't have to learn, you had the knack.'

'We could have started a garage together,' said M. 'You and me. The customers would have been satisfied.'

'Your mother would have put a stop to that. She wouldn't let me come to table covered in oil, until one day she took our Volkswagen to a garage and was faced with the bill. Then she realised how much money I saved with my "tinkering".'

The two of them had got up and without a word had

left the table *and* the house. I was left alone with the remains of the meal and the ruined tablecloth. I must get Gilles out of bed, I had thought. That child had been in bed far too long. Gilles had been well trained too. He didn't dare call out or cry. How long would he stay quietly in his bed? It's not normal, I thought. Children must dare to and be able to make a din if they are hungry or are bored or are wearing a dirty nappy. Tears filled my eyes. Forgive me, darling Gilles, I murmured. But I still sat there as if turned to stone. My child would not have a grandfather. He hadn't even asked after him. That diesel engine interested him more than the child.

I didn't need to make an excursion to the ancestral farmhouse. I knew it, and also the stories about the rich family past. About ten days after we had met, M had driven with me to the farmhouse of the 'ancestors'. That was how I knew I wasn't just a flash in the pan for him, even though he was married and had other girlfriends. 'This here is all ours,' he had said. 'We can do what we like here.' There was a tree growing through the roof and it stank of piss and shit. For how many years had the farmhouse been abandoned? M couldn't say. The decay was a detail. What mattered was that the farmhouse belonged to the family. For generations and generations they worked the land, tamed nature. What land? I wanted to ask, as the farmhouse lay in the middle of a fir wood. We had had to drive half a kilometre along a bumpy dirt road to get there.

'My grandfather broke with tradition. He wanted to take to the skies; I would have liked to be a pilot too, but these'—he tapped his glasses—'frustrated that dream.'

Angrily he kicked an empty beer bottle. 'People have

no respect. If a house is standing empty, they think they can do anything they like.'

He went over to the car and got in. I followed him meekly. As I was about to fasten my safety belt, I saw that he had unbuttoned his trousers. Without looking at him I freed his stiff penis and began sucking him off. I felt so proud. I saw it as a pact, a sacred pact between him and me. Even though I knew that other women sucked him off too. And sometimes I think that if I were sitting again with him in a van in the middle of a wood and he unbuttoned his trousers, I would take his penis in my mouth again. And he would know that I would do it.

When he came, I wound down the window and spat out his sperm, right onto the ancestral grounds. M chuckled. 'There'll be babies growing here soon,' he said.

So this was the spot where the family had its roots.

'My family always turned down a noble title,' said M. 'If you accept a title like that, you recognise the superiority of the person awarding you the title. You give him power over you.'

Don't laugh. I mustn't laugh, certainly not by myself in my cell, otherwise they'll think I've gone crazy. As crazy as Geneviève Lhermitte. Or even crazier.

That isn't possible. She is in a class of her own.

Crazy, but also sly and sharp. Sharper than me. Which isn't difficult, as M would say.

She had to think it all up by herself. She had to think *and* act. Plan *and* execute. I didn't need to plan anything and I wasn't allowed to plan anything. Whenever I planned anything, like the meal for the father, it went wrong, which proved that I was someone who carried out orders. And still am. I learned that lesson, and made sure I didn't forget.

Lhermitte *had* planned it down to the smallest detail. She could not deny it afterwards. There was the knife she had bought, and the letter she had posted through the letter box of a friend, the letter in which she wrote what she had decided to do, and subsequently did. If that friend had found the letter earlier...

If, if, if. M hated 'if'.

If I hadn't gone skating, I wouldn't have met M. My mother forbade me to do virtually everything, but not that. She had skated as a child, on a skating rink, but also on canals and ponds, because there were real winters then with real ice that groaned and creaked. There were photos of her in the album as a skater complete with a grey fur hat with white fur pompoms. Skating was part of life.

'You would have met me,' said M. 'I would have found you.' And he said I should be grateful to him, that I owed everything to him. 'Without me you're nothing.'

'Kiss me. Please.'

Had I begged for a kiss? Yes, I had begged for a kiss.

'You have to earn a kiss, Odette.'

I had tried even harder; Gilles must do his best too. He must understand that his father needed silence, and calm.

Lhermitte's eldest was already fourteen. They're no longer children at that age.

In the eyes of the law they are, though.

All five of them carried and given birth to by her, and perhaps breast-fed too. I don't know, it wasn't in any of the newspapers or magazines that we can read in here. One day she got up and had breakfast with her children. I expect she helped the little ones to brush their teeth and get dressed. Perhaps she took them to school, or perhaps they were picked up by a school bus. Afterwards she went and bought a butcher's knife. They say she didn't pay for it. She slipped it into her bag unnoticed. She didn't declare it at the checkout. The woman wasn't stupid. She didn't want to awaken suspicion. Did she quickly test the blade with her fingertips before she slipped it into her bag? Did she give it an extra sharpen when she got home? Let's hope the knife was sharp, razor sharp. The sharper the knife, the less the pain.

First in line was her little boy, then the youngest girl and so on. The very same children with whom she had had breakfast in the morning, she slaughtered in the afternoon.

It must have exhausted her!

Perhaps she did not cut, but thrust. Thrusting is easier than cutting.

What did she do with the blood that gushed out of their throats? Did she wash it away after each murder? Did she put on clean clothes every time before she went down to lure the next child upstairs?

'Let your hands do the work.' That was what M used to say. 'You mustn't think. You must just do.' He had to be able to rely on my doing something when he asked me, without asking questions. A question was a sign of distrust. And he wouldn't tolerate distrust. 'Forget everything you've ever learned. You're not a schoolteacher here. I give the orders.'

It excited me.

I felt it immediately down there, between my legs. And I nodded. Yes. You're right.

'Do you think it's easy for me?' Sometimes he started hitting me there and then. They were no more than taps to my head, sometimes to my ear. Almost playful, like a lion that is bored, or is warming up for the real work.

'I know it's not easy for you, M, and I respect you in everything that you do. I really respect you.'

'I have to be sure of you.'

'You can be sure of me.'

If I was lucky, the hitting stopped. The taps didn't become slaps or blows, thumping or kicking.

Sometimes he grunted. Then I knew he was satisfied. I knelt at his feet, untied his shoelaces, and pulled off his shoes and socks. I filled a bowl with water—not too hot, not too cold—and put his feet in. I squeezed some soap into the palm of my left hand, lathered his feet with it and massaged them. I even cleaned the gaps between his toes. And if necessary I clipped his toenails. Nice and straight, as I had learned from my father. Toenails must be cut straight, fingernails in an arc. And then they must be filed.

Fingernails grow three times as fast as toenails, no one knows why.

When M relaxed, he even let himself be kissed. I carefully took his glasses off his nose, put my arms round his neck and covered his face with kisses. 'I love you,' I said. 'I love you. I love you.' The same three words again and again, nothing else. Don't think. Don't ask questions. Do.

I meant every word. I had to mean them. He would have known if I hadn't meant them. M could smell lies and hesitation. Something was either black or white. He said that often. 'There's no such thing as grey.'

And he said I mustn't provoke him. Why did I provoke him?

Even when he was in prison and I wasn't, he demanded blind obedience. Prison was a detail for him. He was and would always be the boss.

The female of the species always submits to the male. Otherwise there can be no sex.

'Yes,' I said. 'You're the boss.' And I submitted. I carried out every single order of his. Almost.

6

Anouk disapproves of my interest in Geneviève Lhermitte. My 'pathological, morbid interest,' as she calls it. I would do better to question my own actions. Should she sum them up again?

There's no need. Every paper reminds me, and dreams up new, fresh ones. The greater the chance of my being granted an early release, the more often my misdeeds are listed, and they write that I have no remorse and keep hiding behind excuses, and that I am still not able to confront the truth. 'Let's not forget that this woman held the camera with which she filmed her husband raping helpless women. She gave him instructions. She egged him on.'

Oh yes? Then they know more than I do.

Would I have done it if he had ordered me to?

Probably.

An order from M could not be ignored. Wishes must be respected.

With each order he proved his power over me, the power of imposing his will on me. Each order also proved my power over him, the power of enticing him to exercise that power. He wanted to impose his power on me. I awakened that desire in him, not once, but repeatedly, even when he had been with other women. Especially then.

Perhaps he sought in other women a release from his need to subjugate me, though I was already subjugated. How could he know that with absolute certainty?

'I must be able to be sure of you, Odette.'

'You can be sure of me, M.'

I loved his latent uncertainty. Something in me must have sparked it. One day I shall be—rightly—punished for it.

Which of us two was the sadist? Who pulled the strings? Who drew the long straw? Who got the short one?

My body tingled from top to toe: my blood, my skin, my pores, my cunt. My head became as light as a feather. It's flying away, I thought. I'm flying away.

It still excites me.

What would the papers write if I had admitted that, or if I admit it now?

I will never admit it, never, definitely not to Anouk, especially not to her.

'You needn't concern yourself with Geneviève Lhermitte,' says Anouk. 'You should reflect on yourself. What did you feel when you filmed those rapes? Were you ashamed?'

'Yes,' I say. 'I was ashamed.'

Even if I didn't film those rapes, I was ashamed. I *am* ashamed about what I would have felt *if* I had filmed them: joy, excitement, triumph.

One of his pals is bound to have held the camera. Or they took turns filming and raping. I didn't bother him with questions. I had put my life in his hands. What he did was good.

'Why should you pay for porn when you can make *and* sell your own? You must always make more than you need yourself. You keep the best for yourself, and sell the rest.'

As if he was talking about soup, or about piglets.

For him it was a win-win situation.

What was it for me?

'Do you think I rape women for my pleasure?' he complained. 'Don't you realise I'd prefer to be home sitting quietly in front of the television? Did I ask to have a penis?'

'No, darling.' And I kissed him. He was a man; he had to fuck, subjugate, impose his will. Thanks to me he could be a man. He was my man and he was my son, my brother. How can you understand that, Anouk?

When he said: hire a camera, I hired a camera. If he had ordered me to film, I would have filmed. If he had said: kill the children, our children... If he had said: either you kill them, or I'll do it and afterwards I'll kill you...

He wouldn't have said that. If he thought it should happen, he would have done it himself. Or he would have ordered one of his pals to do it.

I'll say that for him.

And he never used a knife. He had other means. I preferred him not to tell me too much about it. It was his life. Sometimes he needed me to help, and then he told me what to do.

There are leaders and there are followers.

With Lhermitte there were two leaders in the house, she and the doctor who had more or less adopted her husband. She should have got rid of him, not her children. He tried to subdue her, but she fought back like Daniel in the lion's den. There was bound to be a clash, and it was bound to end in tears. Her husband was a follower. He sat comfortably in a plane while his children were being killed—the perfect, watertight alibi. He had been visiting his family in Morocco. The police were waiting for him at the gate. 'We have bad news for you, Sir.' Some homecoming.

'I pray for her,' I say to Anouk about Lhermitte, 'and for her children, and her husband.'

The last statement is a lie.

'And do you pray for your own husband?' she asks.

'M is my ex-husband.'

Let's cross our t's.

What do those bits of paper mean? Those quickly scribbled signatures?

Lhermitte has also divorced her husband. Or he has divorced her. He has recently remarried. New children will come. The father will want to repair what is irreparable.

She and I embraced our misfortune with our eyes open. First we embraced our happiness and then we embraced our misfortune. We have that in common at least.

Are there photos of her children in her cell? Does she beg them for forgiveness?

I, the most hated woman in the country, declare with my hand on my heart that I am not capable of cutting my children's throats. For a start I'm not capable of planning anything. First my mother arranged everything, then M told me what to do.

That will soon become my great challenge, says my psychotherapist, the aforementioned Anouk.

By 'soon' she means: when I am released. I scarcely dare to think those four words: when I am released. I'm frightened I will burst out laughing. Or crow with joy. Me free and not him!

'We don't have the right to judge or condemn our fellow-man,' says Sister Virginie. And then she smiles her Mona Lisa smile.

How does she judge me?

Sometimes I think I'm in love with her, a tiny bit in love.

Lhermitte did it on a Wednesday. Her eldest daughter came home a little late, but when she arrived her mother sat them all in front of the television. It didn't say in the paper what programme they were watching, or which of the five had been allowed to choose the programme. Perhaps they were watching a DVD, perhaps there was a film which all five of them loved and which the mother knew they would stay and watch, whatever happened. She went upstairs, where the knife was ready. One by one she called the children up on some pretext, each time to a different room. She laid the corpse under the duvet in the bed that was standing there, the bed in which she had often kissed them good night.

First there were five of them watching television, then four, then three, then two. Finally only Yasmine was sitting there. Her mother called her too. She was the last to suffer the same fate. Yasmine tried to knock the knife out of her hands. She pushed her mother away, but her mother was stronger than her.

After the fight with her daughter she no longer had the strength to kill herself. She stabbed herself feebly, but did not manage to inflict a fatal wound. Perhaps she didn't want to die.

That woman is not hated. She isn't called a monster. With your own children you can do what you like.

Lhermitte is in prison. That other one, that youth

group leader, who confessed to having smothered her baby with a pillow, is walking round free as a bird. She can come and go whenever and wherever she likes. She'll never become a mother again. No way. She states it in a tone that says: look, I've been punished enough. Soon we'll have to feel sorry for her. Poor baby-murderess who won't have any more children! Who will stop her if she becomes pregnant again? Who will force her to have an abortion? No one has ever taken to the street on her account. And no one has ever demanded that she be put behind bars forever. No one has chanted her name outside the court. No one wonders who is protecting her. People have already forgotten her. I haven't. I keep track of it all. I want to know all the facts about the murderess-mothers. Thanks to Anouk we have Belgian and foreign papers, and magazines on a great variety of subjects. 'Prisoners must not lose touch with the outside world,' she says. 'They must broaden their horizons. Television is not enough.' And the internet is off-limits to us, but that will change sooner or later too. 'Sooner rather than later.' The Minister of Justice has announced that she will investigate at short notice the desirability of limited access to the internet for prisoners. So Anouk says, with an expression as if she were personally heading the investigation.

With a little luck I shan't be around. Investigations like that can easily take a few years.

They will make a positive recommendation, says Anouk. The minister realises that prisoners must stay in touch. They mustn't get the feeling that the world ends at the prison walls.

I've never had that feeling.

I read every word in the paper about the internet, about Google and Facebook and Twitter. 'A waste of time and effort,' in Gilles' opinion. According to him I'll never learn to use it. 'You're too old to learn.'

I don't contradict him. Men can't stand being contradicted. Not even by their mothers.

He seems to have forgotten that his father had computers and that I also worked on them regularly, at first on computers with function keys, then with icons and a mouse. I know perfectly well how to click on things and drag them. I did that often when I had to type out sections of articles that he found interesting, on evolutionary theory, or property investment, or addiction, or DNA research. And M was pretty handy with them too. But we never sent an email or 'surfed' to a website. We had no internet connection. No one had in those days, or at any rate no one we knew. Many people didn't even have a computer. M bought them for a song through a pal of his who was the caretaker of a school where all the computers were thrown out and replaced every five minutes. The school building was about to collapse, the furniture was falling to bits, there was no money to replace the leaking roof, but every year they had new computers. That was the future, the head teacher said. The school had to invest in them. M sold those computers, but always kept a couple back for us, Not for Gilles. Computers aren't toys, he said. There's a time for everything.

The thought of those computers made him terribly nervous when he was in prison, not the first time, because then he didn't yet have any computers at all, which proves that it is true that it's better to live like the lilies of the field. Possessions bring only worries and agitation. Anouk's son lives with a hundred possessions.

He is very rigid and consistent in this, Anouk says. A pair of shoes, a pair of underpants, a pair of socks, a T-shirt and a pair of trousers count as five possessions. In that way you get to a hundred before you know it. A toothbrush, a shaver, a jacket, a handkerchief, a duvet, a wallet, and so on. He only buys something new when he has thrown something old out, or given it away. But he never wants to get rid of his iPad. He'd rather die than trade it in.

Anyway, M was in prison again and I went to visit him. I had brought Elise with me. Gilles and Jérôme were with Ida, the only friendly woman in the entire neighbourhood. I didn't want our sons to be there because I had unpleasant news. M couldn't take out his frustration on them, the warders wouldn't allow it, but the boys could never sit quietly on a chair for long. That annoyed M. I thought: don't add fuel to the fire, this will be a difficult conversation anyway.

I had washed and curled my hair, and put on a blouse he liked, and Elise was wearing a lovely little romper suit. I said to him: I think there's been a break-in at your place. No beating about the bush, in your face. He and I were no longer living in the same house at that point, but I occasionally dropped in at his place to collect the post and create the impression that the house was occupied. It was always quite a job getting the three children into the car. I let Gilles sit in the front, which was not really allowed. I got him to sit on a cushion, to make him look bigger, and he had to look tough 'like a real man'. We were never stopped by the police, or by a customs man, so I think he played his part convincingly. My plucky Gilles, who bravely weathered all the storms. On the back seat I put Elise in the Maxi Cosi, which I had borrowed from Ida, and Jérôme in his car seat, both well secured with safety belts. I put a buggy in the boot for Jérôme, because there are a lot of shops there and often I couldn't find a parking space close to the house. Gilles could push the buggy and I had my hands free for Elise and the bag of baby things and the key. Once everyone was in the car I thrust Gilles' PlayStation into his hands and gave Jérôme a biscuit, as it was over half an hour's journey. And I put on a CD of children's songs. That got on Gilles' nerves, but Jérôme liked it and sang along. 'All the ducklings swimming in the water.... Seven little frogs sat... *Meunier, tu dors, ton moulin va trop vite...*' And often Gilles sang along too, at first rather reluctantly, but he soon got into the spirit.

As soon as I got into M's place, I pulled up the blinds at the front, and when I left I let them down again. M was like my mother in that: the blinds always had to be lowered, otherwise you weren't at ease in your own house. I had a different view, but I followed his instructions. That time I had seen immediately that there was something wrong. The chairs lay higgledy-piggledy over the floor, having been overturned. And there were computers missing. I couldn't keep it from M. I had to tell him.

He went as white as a sheet. 'How many?' he asked. I had never counted the computers, and nor had he. In my opinion there used to be more in the room next to the stairs. Before the break-in you could scarcely move in there, and now you could. Jérôme had sat tapping away at a keyboard with his little fingers. 'Daddy's computers!' Gilles had cried out, pulling his brother away. I didn't mention that last fact to M.

Did I realise how much those computers were worth? he asked, seething.

'But you paid scarcely anything for them!'

Which didn't mean they were worthless. He didn't pay anything for the porn he made either, but he had earned a lot from it. And he had been on the point of doing really profitable business with those computers when he was arrested. It was always the same: the police threw a spanner in the works. He wasn't given a chance. It had been the same when he was a child, when he was hounded from school like a mangy dog, while he had been top of the class, and had been given ninety-six per cent—ninety-six per cent! How many children gained ninety-six per cent of the possible marks? Ninety-six per cent meant that you were exceptionally gifted. You belonged to the elite, together with heavyweights like Einstein, Darwin, Faraday, Oppenheimer, Watson, Crick... In a Communist country you would have had extra instruction because they knew you would eventually do great things, you would bring honour to your country, but he had been rejected, out of jealousy they had...

At that moment I looked at one of the warders. I thought: he'll step in; they can't let him rant like this in the visiting area. He can go on for ages, and very soon no one here will be able to understand each other.

'Look at me when I'm talking to you, Odette.'

For a moment I was frightened he would slap my face there in the visiting area in order to humiliate me, the way his mother had humiliated him with slaps in the face. He would have preferred her to spit, he sometimes said. Spitting is more honest. M spat. He hit and bit and scratched, and he put his loaded revolver next to him on the table with the barrel pointing towards me. I almost wet myself.

I was terrified now too. Had one of his pals managed to smuggle in a revolver for him? Had he done a deal with one of the warders? Had he made it as an informer here too?

With my arm I protected Elise's head. Were we not safe from him even in prison?

Help, I thought. Help me and my child!

I did not dare to try and catch the eye of a warder again. Was he in the plot? Who said I could trust him? Did I have red blotches on my neck? M hated them. 'Are you going through the menopause?' he snapped at me. 'Has it come to that?'

My fear made him suspicious. 'Did you sell those computers?'

'Who to?'

'I don't know, Odette. I'm in prison. I do my best to keep control, but I can't keep track of everything, especially not when you don't take responsibility and let people break in. If you sold those computers and put the money in your pocket, it would be better to admit it now. I'm prepared to be understanding. I may even forgive you. Just possibly I'll let you keep part of the money. I realise it's not easy for you.'

'Don't you trust me then, the mother of your children?'

'If I were to trust all the mothers of my children...'

'How can you say a thing like that?'

I took my hand from Elise's face and showed him his child, his daughter. 'She's smiling already. Smile at your Daddy. Shush shush, don't cry, there's no need to cry, Mummy's with you, and Daddy.'

He didn't even look at her. 'I'm realistic, Odette. It's time you learned to be realistic too. Tell me the truth.'

'Have I ever lied to you?'

'How can I know that?'

'What do I have to do to make you believe me?'

'You can't do anything. What you can do is accept that you can't do anything.'

I shook my head in disbelief. 'I've done everything for you. Everything! I've never refused you anything.'

'But it's not enough.'

'What should I have done then?'

'Made sure that I trusted you.'

'I gave you a daughter,' I whispered with my head bowed. 'Won't you take her in your arms?

'I don't feel it,' he said. 'I don't feel I can trust you, I don't feel that she is my daughter. Why don't I feel it?'

If we had been at my place or his I would have thrown myself at his feet to prove my loyalty. His distrust hurt more than anything. It was a betrayal of everything that was between us. He and I had so often been a team. We had driven miles and miles in that clapped-out van to collect scrap, or to go and test a car, or to find a woman for him. I had never complained, not even that time we had had to run far too fast away from the bank where we had tried to withdraw money from a savings book that he and his mates had stolen. He was lucky that I was there, because I had seen the bank clerk reach for a button under the counter and press it. I was sure it was an alarm. M afterwards admitted that he had misjudged the situation, and that it could have had dramatic consequences. Thanks to me we escaped. Just like Bonnie and Clyde.

For the last few years I had hardly ever been out on a job with him. Gilles needed lots of attention, my health was poor, I had no child care for the little ones, *and* we agreed that I had to stay out of prison. My mother was getting older, and we could no longer count on her for the children. Increasingly M relied on friends, or people who were in his debt, or who wanted drugs and didn't know how to get hold of them. M knew, he knew everything. Perhaps he and I had become estranged. He now seemed to be on the point of denying his paternity, exactly as *his* father did and had done. That was quite a blow.

'Look at her,' I begged. 'Please. She's so sweet.'

He didn't react.

'She looks like you, M.'

'Have you been drinking coffee again? You needn't reply, I can tell from everything, you've been drinking coffee. We agreed you wouldn't drink coffee.'

'During my pregnancy.'

'You're lying, Odette. It's embarrassing when you lie.'

'Forgive me. Please.'

'There's no point. It goes on and on. You keep making the same mistake.'

'If you like, I won't come and visit you anymore.'

He ignored that remark, which anyway was totally idiotic.

'Give me a chance, M. Please.'

Elise began crying and I was snivelling too.

'Go away,' he said. 'I really don't need this. You have to earn trust. Prove I can trust you.'

'What do I have to do?'

'You know what you have to do.'

He had given me a last chance. The agreement was clear: the computers that were left must be protected. He accepted that a number of computers had been lost but the loss must be restricted. That is where I could show my responsibility and my loyalty. I must take Brutus and Nero to his house to deter burglars. 'Otherwise they'll come back,' he said. 'They always come back when they've scored a success. I've done it myself. You think: I know that house, I know where the weak points are, *and* where the loot is.'

How was I to get the dogs there? Brutus and Nero weren't small dogs, they were Alsatians. They wouldn't both fit into the car.

'Who will feed them?' I asked. I didn't want to be difficult, I wanted to show my gratitude, but I needed more instructions.

'You,' he said. 'Who else?'

'And the children?' I saw myself arriving there with three children and tins of dog food and newspapers for their droppings.

'What children?'

'Our children. How can I look after them *and* the dogs?'

'You're doing that anyway, aren't you?' It's just that the dogs will be in my house instead of yours.'

'They can't be shut up there day and night.'

'Why not? I'm shut up here day and night.'

'That's different.'

'Why?'

'You're being looked after.'

'The dogs will be looked after too, by you.'

'Brutus gets claustrophobic if he can't go out. And Nero will howl the whole time if I leave him alone there without Brutus.'

'You must pop in once or twice a day to walk the dogs.'

'With the children?'

'With the children or without them. Use your brain. It's not that difficult, is it?'

I swear that he did not say a word at that time about the other children, the children they say were in the cellar. I won't exclude the possibility that he was thinking of them, and perhaps the thought of them flashed through my head for a second, but I doubt it. We were concerned about the dogs and the computers, which had to be guarded. I would have liked to suggest moving the computers to my place, but I had no room. I really couldn't fit them in: a house isn't a warehouse. And I couldn't put them in the yard: they would get ruined in the rain and wind.

Computers have changed, says Anouk. You can't compare today's computers with the old monsters you used to have. No one uses them any more.

M won't be pleased to hear that.

My Gilles knows more about computers than his father now. Recently he was given an iPad in exchange for an interview. In that way the newspaper could maintain that they didn't pay him. 'I have the sensitivity of my mother and the intelligence of my father,' he said in that interview, and that he visits his father more frequently than me.

That made me cry. Who cared for him? Who comforted him when his father snapped at him? Who helped him with his homework? Who cooked meals for him? Who knitted sweaters for him? I would still be knitting sweaters for him, but he won't wear them anymore. The last one I knitted he wouldn't even try on. Ungrateful boy!

'M is his father and always will be,' Anouk says.

He is the only one of the three who can remember how little attention that father paid to his children, and how free he was with his hands and fists.

He couldn't stand anything to do with the children. Not a thing. He couldn't even stand a baby monitor. 'We don't need a baby monitor,' he said. 'With a baby monitor you only encourage them to cry. You charge up to their room at the first peep they give. I want peace and quiet. In orphanages there's no crying. Why? Because the children know that crying is pointless. Even the babies know that.'

'Our children aren't orphans.'

'Not for now,' he said.

I walked round for long nights with Gilles at my breast to calm him down. Softly I sang one song after another. Songs occurred to me that I hadn't sung for years. I walked for miles with that child in my arms so that his lordship could sleep, in spite of the fact that the doctors had said that *I* needed rest.

Children think they know everything, but they haven't got a clue.

I don't blame Gilles. I can understand, but it's hurtful, for my mother too, who looked after him so often, when circumstances prevented us from doing so. We couldn't call on M's family. None of them ever said: Odette, you have to go to the prison. Who's going to look after Gilles? Or: Odette, you've been classified as an invalid. Do you need help? I've often been on the point of writing Gilles a letter telling him the truth, but Anouk says that he has the right to his own story. Everyone has a right to it.

'And the truth?' I said. 'It has its claims too.'

'You always have to be right.'

'That's what M said.'

She went bright red. One moment she was pale, the next bright red. I looked down in embarrassment, and apologised for my rudeness.

'Perhaps I shall have to revise my opinion of you,' she said. But she didn't sound angry. Almost the reverse.

Shortly afterwards she promised me she would teach me to use the internet, on her computer. Not now, but when I was released. She predicted that I would pick it up quickly. Almost everyone has a computer today, she said, or a smartphone. Thanks to touchscreens children can use a computer long before they can read or write.

All those new words: smartphone, touchscreen.

In some schools they don't use exercise books anymore. Every child has a laptop, or an iPad. Some children have to go into therapy as young as ten to kick a computer addiction.

'Young people scarcely phone each other anymore. They chat via Facebook. They're always online.'

Chatting. Online. When I'm released I can go online too, and chat. M will die without ever having been online, or having chatted.

Anouk says: 'If I were you, I wouldn't type in my name.'

She means: on Google, or another search engine. But almost everyone uses Google. And they say: I'll google it.

I wonder if Gilles has already googled me? Or his father? Does Anouk google me?

She looks at my folders full of paper clippings. My 'morbid' folders.

'Some people feel less inhibited on the internet. I think you'd rather not read what some people would like to do to you, if they had the chance.'

'It's in the papers too.'

'It's worse on the net. Everything is worse on the net. The internet brings out the worst in human beings.'

Worse than what? I think. Worse than sixteen years in prison? Worse than being reviled by everyone?

Paedophiles hunt for a prey on the internet now. I cut out that article for Elise, and told her she must be careful, very careful. I made her swear never to tell anyone who her parents are. 'Never give it away, Elise. Even if you think you can trust someone. You can't trust anyone. That is my fault and your father's. I know. I would give anything to undo it, but I can't.'

I wanted to tell her that she could only trust God, but the word means nothing to her.

'Gilles and Jérôme know who I am,' she said.

'They're your brothers.'

'And Alain knows.'

'Alain?'

'Your lawyer.'

'You call him Alain?'

'That's his name.'

'You must be polite, Elise. We can't afford to be impertinent. Mr Moyson will keep quiet.'

'I'll keep quiet too, Mummy. You needn't be afraid.'

I thought of the crazy woman who had silenced her children with a knife.

'Swear,' I said to Elise. 'Swear that you'll keep quiet.' I put two fingertips on her lips, pushing away the thought of the murderess. Then I made her kneel facing the crucifix. I took the Bible and placed her hand on it.

'Mummy!'

'It doesn't matter that you don't believe. I believe.'

'I shall never tell anyone who I am.'

'You must swear.'

'I swear I will never tell anyone who I am.'

'Not even for money,' I said.

'Not even for money,' she repeated.

'Nor for an iPad.'

'Nor for an iPad.'

I knelt beside her and prayed. Always the same prayer: don't let anyone ever take revenge on my children.

An eye for an eye, a tooth for a tooth, a child for a child.

While I was praying I took hold of her hand. She didn't pull it away. She never pulls it away. Elise is the baby they tore from my arms. She had two teeth and could already crawl. In my mind I called her the-baby-who-follows-me-around-everywhere. But afterwards she became the-baby-they-tore-from-my-arms.

Nine months in my belly and nine months in my arms. Nine months and three weeks.

The first few months count double, perhaps even treble.

M held her in his arms once at most. She was scarcely eight days old when he was arrested. Car theft. They take no account of the family situation. Baby or no baby: straight into the cell. He thought that they would leave him alone over such a trifle. He said that literally: a trifle. 'Listen,' he said, 'I perform lots of services for the police for which they can't pay me officially. So they let me take what I need and look the other way.'

I didn't want to know about it, but anyway I was left behind alone with three children. And my mother was already no longer up to it. I had scarcely any help from her. I gave the baby love enough for two. And my sons were also given double portions of love by me. Tell them that in an interview, Gilles!

M wanted children, but they mustn't make a noise and most of all they mustn't cost anything. His father was the same. He stole his children's pocket money. What father does that? When the children were given something by a Granddad or a Granny, they had to surrender it. He would look after it. Or pay it into the bank. In exchange they were given a piece of paper with the amount owing on it, which they never saw again. M learned very early how to earn money for himself, and especially how to hide it carefully. I don't think he ever took money from Gilles. We didn't give Gilles any pocket money, but my mother probably slipped him something now and again. I don't know what he did with it. Bought sweets, I assume.

A mother cannot know everything about her children, and doesn't need to know everything, but she can expect a little gratitude, at least if she's fought as hard for her children as I have.

M's mother calls M her ex-son.

I couldn't do that. Whatever the children do, they remain your children, certainly for the mother, who has given birth to them and cannot possibly doubt her maternity.

Well, M expected nothing more from his mother, absolutely nothing. 'She hated me and I hated her. In that respect we were well matched. She would have done better to throw me in a river in the Congo and say it was an accident. She could have had me eaten by a crocodile. She was jealous of me because Granny loved me and looked after me well. I regard Granny as my real mother. Not my mother.'

They that sow the wind shall reap the whirlwind.

The father tried to make things right. He felt so guilty about the Cain complex he had inflicted on his son that he gave him his car. Just like that. He had decided he no longer wanted a car and he wouldn't have got much for it anyway, but still he did it. M was so overwhelmed he went searching for his father's golden chess medal he had stolen. 'I'll give it back,' he said. And he gave it back. I just mean: there's a good side to M. People don't always realise, but he does have one. He was the only one in the family who cared for Granny, or tried to. From prison he arranged as much as he could for her. He spent hours on the telephone with her. He nagged the prison governor endlessly until he was given one day's leave from prison to go and clean at her place under strict escort. The woman let her cats piss and shit everywhere. That house was filthy! I didn't want to set foot in it again. I already had Gilles, I couldn't run the risk of his contracting a disease that might not be dramatic for cats, but was for a child. You can't be too careful. AIDS began as a disease of monkeys, and look what happened. Everyone was afraid of diseases and infections, and no one could stand the stench, but M defied all that. He scraped the cat shit off the floor with a knife on his hands and knees. He could not live with the thought that his Granny had to live in filth. His mother couldn't be bothered. It finished up with *me* taking his Granny—*her* mother, that is—to live with me. I did that with pleasure, since I knew how important she had been for M. The tiny bit of sun he had known in his childhood came from her. And he was the sun to her.

And for me too.

First he was the sun, then a boiling volcano. Worse than a volcano.

Elise has promised me solemnly that when she comes of age shortly she will not visit her father, even though she is allowed to.

I made her swear that too on her knees in front of the crucifix.

'There's nothing for you there. You know what he did while you were in my tummy.'

'I know, Mummy.'

'And you know what he did when he came out of

prison and you were a baby scarcely four months old.'

'Yes, Mummy, I know.'

'He had no respect at all for you, and I don't want you ever to have any respect for him.'

Then she said that she had seen a photo of me with M on the internet. 'You look very happy, and in love. Daddy is wearing dark glasses. You can't see his eyes, but yours are shining with happiness.'

'Don't call him "Daddy".'

'What do I call him then?'

I shrugged my shoulders.

'Were you happy then, Mummy?'

I nodded. There was no point in denying it. For months I was the happiest woman in the world. I kissed my fingertips, thrust my arms in the air and thanked heaven. I had escaped, I had escaped, I had escaped!

And I chattered. Sophie the crocodile, who chatters on, who chatters on, Sophie the crocodile, her mouth moves all the while. I told him everything. About my father, my mother, my Grannies and Granddads, cousins, about the candle that lay on my bedside table supposedly in case there was a power cut, and with which I played when I was sure my mother was asleep, about the lipstick that I smuggled out of the house hidden in my vagina, as it was the only place where my mother wouldn't look for it, about the assistant in the lingerie shop who stayed in the fitting room and 'helped' me try on bras. About how I took off one bra and waited a long time before trying the other, much longer than was necessary. How we smiled shamelessly at each other in the mirror. But mainly I told him about my mother and how I hated her, how I was afraid I would no longer be able to keep the hatred hidden, that I would shout it from the rooftops, that one day, without remorse or regret, I would hit her, or strangle her, or spit in her face. I showed him how I imitated her in the mirror in my room. Can you go crazy with hatred?

'Of course,' he said.

I took a lipstick and stuck it inside me. First I took the top off and then I stuck it inside me. I squatted and demonstrated how I could draw a face on the sheet in lipstick. He laughed, I laughed, and we rolled on the bed laughing. I took the lipstick and showed him how I caressed myself with it. Then I painted my lips *there*. Kiss me, I said. I pressed his head towards my bright red lips, my lips had to colour his lips red, and most of all he had to lick me. But he pushed my head towards his penis, which was as hard as steel. I applied lipstick to my lips, the lips of my mouth, and coloured his penis as red as fire. While I sucked and sucked, I ran the lipstick, which had once been in my mother's handbag, back and forth over my clitoris, which swelled and swelled and he too swelled in my mouth and I thought: come, come, because I knew I would not be able to go on sucking if I came, I would fall on the bed like a wet rag. He stroked his balls and I knew: it can happen any moment now, I mustn't stop sucking now, in a moment the fireball will explode in me. First he began shaking, then I did, but I shook for much longer than he did: I lay on the bed shaking like an epileptic. There were red smears on the sheet from the lipstick, and on his belly and mine too, and he laughed and said he had not been wrong, that I was the sexiest, horniest babe in the whole country, and that he would buy me a new lipstick, as the tip had broken off this one, and I said he would have to steal one out of my mother's handbag or out of her make-up box, and he said: when are you going to do that?—and I said: now, and he got dressed and I got dressed, and so he and I drove to my mother's house with that smell of sex on our bodies, we reeked of sex for miles around, and I introduced him to her. I said: 'Look, Mummy, this is the man I told you about.' For a moment I actually loved her, I loved everything and everyone, and I thought: everything will be all right now, because there's a new man in our family, Mummy will learn to appreciate and love him as I do, at last she'll be able to forget my father. M asked where the toilet was, but I heard him go upstairs and so did my mother. 'He's got no business upstairs,' she screamed. She was about to chase after him, but I stopped her. 'He wants to see the bedroom,' I said. 'He wants to see where I slept for all those years. I'm so happy, Mummy.' I hugged her, *I* hugged my mother. She pushed me away. 'Idiot' she said, she didn't want an idiot in her house and that man must get out too, where did he get the cheek to snuffle round her house, and what did I know about the man? What did he do for a living? Was it true he was married? Really true? Or had I said it to wind her up? 'It's true,' I said. 'He's married but he's going to get divorced. He loves me now. I'll become his children's stepmother!' Again I tried to hug her, again she pushed me away. The door opened. M raised his clenched fist. In it was the loot: a lipstick of my mother's', Lancôme, it turned out later. It fitted not only in my vagina, but also in my arse.

'Come on,' said M. 'We've been here long enough.'

Then of course she wanted us to stay. We couldn't go without having a drink. What would we like to drink?

M simply walked out of the house. 'Where are you going?' she cried in panic. She tried to stop me. I mustn't go with that man. Men often promised young women that they would divorce. I was naïve and stupid. I didn't know the world, she did. And now I sometimes think: if only she had stopped me. But the truth is that nothing and no one could have stopped me.

That photo must have been taken at that time. Everyone kept saying how good I looked. 'Look in the mirror,' they said. 'You're radiant!' I didn't have to look in the mirror. I could see from the way he looked at me. He couldn't take his eyes off me, definitely when I walked naked through the house. I didn't need any foreplay. His eyes on my body were the foreplay.

Fortunately he didn't take any photos of me; otherwise I'd be on the internet in my birthday suit now.

I think I know which photo Elise meant. A woman friend of mine took it. 'Now you're finally off the streets,' was her comment. And she said it wasn't a problem that he was married and had two sons; a divorce was no longer a disgrace, and was easily arranged.

Elise would do better to do her homework instead of spying on her mother on the internet.

M is monitored day and night in his cell. He is checked every seven minutes. They want to prevent him committing suicide.

A day has 1440 minutes. That means that he is monitored 205 times a day. Almost 9 times an hour.

Whom does it drive mad, him or the warders?

It would be better if they let him commit suicide. 'Here's a rope, hang yourself. Or a knife: you can choose which artery to cut. Come on, we'll give you a hand.'

They could let Lhermitte loose on him.

Anouk knows how I feel about it. Even Sister Virginie knows. She, the saint, who sees the good in everyone, says not a word in his defence.

Perhaps she thinks what I think. That he is the devil. The Antichrist.

There are women who write him love letters. Even now everything about him is known, there are women who are crazy about him.

I should never have given away any secrets about myself. Not a word.

He said it wasn't normal for a girl to play with herself, especially not with a candle. He said I was lucky to have ended up with him. Another man would have rejected me. Normally you had to teach girls to touch themselves. They didn't even know they could stick a finger in themselves, let alone a candle. Or a lipstick. You had to teach them with great patience. It was blood, sweat and tears. Lots of tears. Afterwards they were grateful to you. Once they were used to it, you could stick anything inside them. You had to get them used to it one step at a time, as he had done with me and my arse. First a Lancôme lipstick, then one from L'Oréal, then Chanel, Elizabeth Arden, Dior ... I've had every make in my bum. Then it was the turn of candles. Finally, as the crowning glory, his penis. And he said I was lucky he didn't have a whopping great penis like those porn actors who turned me on. What normal woman gets a wet pussy when she watches porn? If I absolutely wanted a whopper like that in my arse, he would oblige. He would buy me the biggest dildo he could find. He would personally stick it in my arse. Anything to please madame!

And anything to please monsieur. I covered his penis with kisses. 'It's so beautiful,' I said. 'And just the right size. When I watch porn, my pussy gets wet for you!'

And of course with the lipstick in my cunt I had to draw faces for him, pouting faces, faces with tears, heads with hair, without hair, with a hat, with a flower on the hat.

'You ask for it yourself,' he said. 'You must learn to take responsibility. Who started talking about lipstick?'

It wasn't me but him who was the crocodile. He swallowed me up, and spat me out so that he could swallow me up again. All my fault, he said. I had challenged him. Had I expected him to listen like a tame sheep to my smutty tales?

Anouk says: 'M is past tense for you. Now you must reflect on your own actions.'

My non-actions: I am the woman who did not go down into the cellar to feed the abducted girls while their abductor, my husband, was in prison. He had explicitly told me to. He had also said that if I didn't feed them, his pals would do it. W? I thought. But no, that was impossible, W was dead. He lay among the wrecked cars in the cold, churned-up earth of my backyard. What had W done that meant he had to die? Something, I didn't want to know what. Now I couldn't believe my ears. Elise had just been born. I wanted to celebrate my daughter. Our daughter. And he tells me he had abducted two girls and is keeping them in the cellar of his house. He had told me that before, but now he told me as well that if anything happened to him, I must look after them. 'But we're going on a trip,' I said. 'In the mobile home. You promised.'—'Odette, if I'm in prison, we shan't be going on a trip.'

'Why do you have to go to prison?' I began to cry. I had had enough. There was nothing, absolutely nothing left of our marriage.

'Perhaps I'll have to go to prison, perhaps not.'

Eight days later we knew the result. It wouldn't be for long, he said. Four or five months at most.

Four or five months.

I knew that cellar. It was a low, damp cellar, totally unsuited for keeping children in. At the slightest rainfall it flooded. M had once installed a pump to get rid of the water, but it was broken. It had never worked properly. It was typical trash of M's, which he had been able to pick up on the cheap and which was worthless. I couldn't believe that those children were down there. But I knew he was capable of it. That man was capable of anything. I wasn't. I couldn't go downstairs and feed those children. There was a cupboard in front of the entrance that I had to push aside, but I couldn't, I simply couldn't. Perhaps I should have asked Gilles, but no, that wouldn't have worked. Gilles was only eleven, not much older than those girls. He wouldn't have understood what those girls were doing there. I didn't understand either. How could I have explained it?

I carried out all the other instructions scrupulously. Almost all the others.

I fed the dogs. That's in all the papers. Who am I to contradict them? No one ever wonders where the dogs relieved themselves. Or what their names were. The dogs have no name. They were called 'dog'. They lived in the house, the house with the cellar with the girls in it. They walked restlessly to and fro. They barked, they howled, they growled. They were given food by me, food I brought them.

I have read so much about those dogs that I can see them in that house. Two large, black, skinny dogs, with penises. The dogs in M's house have penises. Their ears are ravaged. Other dogs have bitten them to pieces, but they emerged as undisputed victors from every fight. Like their master.

They're not in the least like my dear Brutus and Nero,

whom M told me to take to his house to guard his computers, but that was another order I didn't carry out. How could I shut Brutus and Nero up in there? They would have howled day and night, certainly Brutus, who was the most affectionate of the two and had been with me ever since he was a puppy, when I had bottle-fed him. And fortunately Ida took him in when M and I were arrested in front of the children. He was happy there for a few months. Then someone found out he was my dog and they shot him. Cowards. They can be proud of themselves. Nero was put down in the sanctuary. The staff didn't want to keep him. I felt very guilty about that.

I see myself too. I'm standing at the door of the house, I'm looking for the key. I turn it in the lock. I push the door open cautiously, frightened that the dogs will leap on me. I recoil at the stench.

I don't see the children. I see myself, the dogs, the door, the house.

M liked animals more than human beings, his mother said in an interview. In the past tense. As if he was dead. 'He'd stop and get out for an animal in the road.'

I would be lying if I said I had ever experienced that.

She may have done.

She said nothing in defence of her son, or of me. My father-in-law did, but she didn't.

If M had not been in prison, I would have carried out every order. I would have played the role he had dreamed up for me. Dogs or no dogs, I would have gone into the house with a saucepan of food in my hand and taken it to the children. I would have asked for precise instructions, so I didn't have to think. What if I can't shift the cupboard aside? What if the children attack me? What if they rush past me outside? Do I cook something special for them or do they eat the same as us? Do I stand and wait till their plates are empty? Can I give them cutlery? A fork, a knife? Should I let them go to the toilet? Should I wash them? Wash their clothes? What if they get ill? Get a temperature? A nasty cough? What if they don't like the food? He would have answered all those questions, even before I had asked them.

People write newspaper articles without thinking. They write 'dogs', but don't ask themselves what dogs: how big, how strong, how noisy? They don't ask themselves what a house smells like that dogs have been shut up in for months. Two dogs and two children, yes, but also two dogs, black, gruesome, emaciated, harried-looking dogs.

What journalists don't realise either, or don't know, or don't want to know, is that the mains water supply to the house had been cut off. In order to give everyone food and drink, I would have had to fill a jerry can with water at home and lug it there.

I'm not Hercules!

And all that time M was in prison, again. When I went to visit him people could eavesdrop on us from the other tables, and so could the warders. Sometimes I sat and breast-fed Elise. 'Do you have to do that here?' M said. Of course I had to do it there. She was hungry. Jérôme lay full length on the floor playing with his toy cars. Gilles was sitting beside me on a chair with the PlayStation my mother had bought him. He didn't look at his father, he looked at his PlayStation. If it had been at home M would immediately have taken the Play-

Station away from him. Meanwhile I had to try and listen to what M was saying. 'Feed them,' he said. Who did he mean: our children? The children in the cellar? Of course he meant the children in the cellar. But how? Tell me how? Should I take our three with me to feed those two?

I had to pull up the blinds and let them down again, I had to take his post with me, I had to ensure there wasn't another break-in and that the children didn't break anything.

Enough is enough.

Sometimes I lay down on his bed, with the children. Five minutes' rest. Closing my eyes for five minutes.

It would have been easier if he had got me to have the water turned on again, or if he had arranged it himself. Those kinds of things can be fixed from prison. And if it doesn't work, you submit an application to social services. I didn't have to explain that to him, did I? He'd been in prison longer than I had.

He always thought he was smarter than the police. I thought so too for a long time, because I wanted to. If I hadn't believed it I would have gone crazy. And I mustn't go crazy. My children needed me. They need me.

7

M wanted me because he wanted a daughter. That was one of the first things he said to me in that caravan of his that he had stationed in the car park by the skating rink. And he asked me if I wanted to know how many women he had fucked in that caravan, and how many girls. 'I don't need to know that,' I said calmly. That was lucky, he said, because he didn't know even approximately. 'People have to fuck,' he whispered in my ear. 'Fuck a lot. There's too little fucking.' But despite that fucking he still had no daughter, though he really longed for one. 'Not to fuck,' he said. 'Hahaha,' and I laughed too: 'Hahaha.' Who fucks his daughter when he can have any woman in in the world?

His first wife had given him sons and now he wanted daughters. He had seen me skating with my cousins, and he had thought: that's someone who'll bring only girls into the world. No boys can grow in there. He thought boys were too wild. They broke things and were disobedient. They were stubborn and headstrong. He wanted a girl. When I was pregnant and the gynaecologist had established that it was a boy, he forced me to walk up and down the stairs all evening. He stood at the top and watched me come upstairs. I wasn't allowed to hold the bannisters. Every time I turned to go back downstairs, I was afraid he would push me. He could have pushed me, but he didn't. Perhaps he was proud of making boys so easily. If he really hadn't wanted the baby, he would have found a remedy. M always got his own way.

I wasn't allowed to buy Pampers. He had seen a programme on television about Tibet, where toddlers go around in pants with an open crotch. Everyone can see their bare bottoms. And babies too wear pants with the crotch not sewn up. I should make some pants like that for Gilles, he said.

'No,' I said. 'I'm not doing that.'

Then I was supposed to take old sheets and cut them up into nappies.

'We haven't got any old sheets,' I said.

I don't know where I got the cheek. When it came to the children, I was prepared to take risks. I knew from his first wife that he had tried on the business of those pants with an open crotch with her children too. 'He's a miser,' she had told me. 'He keeps everything for himself. If you ever get a present from him, treasure it, because it won't happen a second time. Most probably it won't happen the first time either, but you may be lucky. At a certain moment he even rationed toilet paper. Not for himself, but for us. We were only allowed to flush once a day.'

When I was pregnant with Gilles I tried to put money aside. I wanted to build a little nest egg for when the baby arrived. At his birth I had scarcely enough for a box of Pampers. He checked everything. He knew the prices and went through all the bills. I wouldn't have dared to buy anything that we had not previously agreed on. How could I save anything?

Anouk says: 'I wouldn't want to put up all the women who have to start a secret savings fund to be able to feed their children, or who have to beg from their parents.'

'Why is that?' I asked her.

She shrugged. 'Many men want children, but they're not prepared to make any sacrifices for them. They want them the way they want a car, and a house, or a watch. More as possessions, or status symbols.'

'Why don't they tell us that at school?'

'Because otherwise no one would start a family. There are different men, but I have never met them. Men want to be at their ease. Women must ensure they can be at their ease. You either accept it or you don't.'

'My father looked after me. He gave all his wages to my mother. She gave him pocket money every week, which he used to spoil her and me.'

'Then your mother was a very lucky woman.'

'First she was lucky, then she was unlucky.'

My mother used to have those big leather purses. They were almost small handbags, big enough to hold a fortune. For my eighteenth birthday she bought me a purse like that too, but I never used it. She assumed I would be like her, and then I would have a daughter who would be like me, and hence like her. And so on and on forever.

She often pointed out to me a flat to let close by. I could live in that later. It was within walking distance of her house. We'd be able to meet every day. She noted down the telephone number of the estate agent and rang for information. 'It's seventy-five square metres,' she was able to tell me, for example, 'with central heating, a fitted kitchen, a large bedroom and a store room, which could be used as a bedroom.' My mother thought that was sufficient for a start. She and my father had started out small too. If you started small you could expand, grow. Once she made an appointment to view a flat which she knew very well neither she nor I would rent. But she wanted to stay abreast of the property market. And she wanted to know the prices. 'Listen,' she said, 'you must never rent a furnished flat. It may sound attractive, but it's far too expensive. Owners furnish it with their own old junk. It's better if you slowly but surely save for your own things.' Or she said: 'A balcony is a must. You can put out a table and chairs, and have breakfast on it, or lunch.' Or: 'Never rent a flat in a building with a caretaker. You pay through the nose for them, and all they do is stick their noses in your business.' And: 'When you're about thirty you should buy something. If you're still renting by that time, something's gone wrong.' She described the flat in which she had lived with my father when they were first married. 'We rented a floor in an ordinary house. There was only one toilet for all the occupants. I'm not ashamed of it. There was a housing shortage at the time. Whole districts had been bombed flat. We couldn't be fussy. We slowly worked our way up.'

If she had seen all the houses that M bought, she would have had a heart attack. What she had seen she thought was bad enough. And how was it possible, how on earth was it possible that such things existed?

My mother sometimes pointed out houses with windows and doors that had the paint peeling off. Or front gardens that were used as rubbish tips. 'Sad, isn't it?' And she said that a house must be at least six metres wide. She could estimate the width of a house front with the naked eye. 'That's not six metres,' she sometimes said with a shake of her head, as if she had accurately measured it. She had accurately measured it, with eagle eyes.

Anouk has seen my house, on Street View, the last house where I lived with the children before I was arrested, and the address of which was given in all my statements. 'You can see that it's been a farmhouse,' she says. I ask her what Street View is and she explains patiently to me, as she explains everything patiently. 'How could you live there?' I say nothing. 'That isn't a house, it's a hovel.' I still say nothing. Maybe it was a hovel, but it had a long front. Not on the street side, but the side wall was over six metres long.

'He planned to do it up further,' I say. 'He wanted to do up all the houses he owned one day. But that cost money and time. Everything costs money, lots of money, and time.'

Anouk goes on looking at me in disbelief.

'Anyway, he invested a lot in that house. The roof leaked and had to be replaced. He took the opportunity to raise it. He and I did that together.'

Jérôme was growing in my belly at the time. I thought M was trying to provoke a miscarriage, because it was a boy again. I had a haemorrhage and went to the doctor. He said I should rest. Doctors always said that I should rest. How could I rest?

'And so it was in that garden that...'

'I had nothing to do with the garden. It was a yard, not a garden. I was the tenant. I rented the house, not the garden, the yard.'

'The bodies of the children were found in that garden, Odette, and the remains of W.'

I lower my eyes, thinking: so they say. So they write.

Gilles also talked about that garden in his interview, about how vividly he remembered the police helicopter landing in the garden. And the armed policemen who were suddenly there. As if he had found it exciting.

The most famous garden in Belgium. The most famous yard.

M won't find it funny that anyone can simply inspect all his houses on Street View just like that. He will write letters demanding a ban, and he will try to lodge a complaint.

He would be right. All that fuss about his houses. Nothing but envy and jealousy! People would do better to mind their own business.

M didn't want any snoopers. If I dared ask him an indiscreet question, he would say: 'You sound like your mother.' The worst thing was that I had usually heard it myself.

'Belgium is full of hovels,' he said. 'A hovel doesn't have to stay a hovel. You've got to think long-term. I've often had to sleep in rooms without windows. I didn't like it, but it didn't kill me. It toughened me up.'

Belgium was an interesting country for people with patience. You had to start small and work your way up, slowly but surely. Each hovel, he said, is a potential goldmine.

My mother had money and that money was in those big purses, and it was in the bank. After my father's death my mother received money from the insurance. She wouldn't tell me how much, but she insinuated constantly that it was an impressive sum, so impressive that it could be spoken of solely in conversations with the bank manager, and then only in a whisper. I had to keep a certain distance, so it could not reach my ears. That was to protect me. What I didn't know, I couldn't blab about, not even, for example, to her sister, who was green with jealousy and employed devious means in the hope of wheedling part of the amount out of her, although she had her husband and unlike my mother was not all alone. 'Is it my fault,' Mummy said, 'that *her* husband didn't have an accident? If I could choose between my husband and the money, I know what I would choose. Or better: who. Money doesn't make you happy, Odette.'

'No, Mummy.'

'But money can ease the pain.'

'Yes, Mummy.'

She didn't let me forget for a second that the amount existed and that one day I would be responsible for it. Then I would learn of its size. She talked constantly about the money, which she had invested wisely on the advice of the bank manager, so that it produced a good yield. My mother's earnings were for fixed overheads. She counted them on her fingers: gas, water, electricity, telephone, insurance, petrol, clothes, food, drink, maintenance. One for each finger. Thanks to the interest we could afford extras. Occasionally my mother was obliged to dip into the capital, for example to buy a new car, or a new three-piece suite, or fashionable frames for her glasses. 'Your father would have wanted it. Or: 'Your father wouldn't want me to go on driving round in that clapped-out car.'

When I met M, I had to swear that after her death I wouldn't give him a franc of my inheritance. If I did, I would be spitting on my father's grave, and on hers.

She nibbled away at the capital more and more often, since I would only squander it on 'that man'. Suddenly I saw her with a Louis Vuitton handbag. Or there was Dior perfume in the bathroom. In the past she would have bought two bottles, one for me and one for her, but I was no longer worth Dior, and certainly not Louis Vuitton.

As a child I hated those conversations about the money, and I hated the money. My mother's investments didn't interest me. I didn't want to know anything about them. At the same time I was pleased that we had money. My father was caring for us through the money that was in the bank or was invested. We often went from my father's grave to the bank. My mother had a safe deposit box for her jewels and shares and Krugerrands, and we went to look at them. If the bank manager was there he always popped in to say hello, and pressed the button which unlocked the safe depository. It was he who told me that banks have an alarm button in the counter. If the bank manager was not there a bank employee unlocked the depository. Sometimes we had to wait because someone else was already inside. Then we sat on chairs next to a tub of plants under a convex mirror. My mother held her handbag firmly on her lap and looked straight ahead of her. I looked from my shoes to the mirror and back at my shoes. Once we were in the depository, my mother took the key out of her bag. She shielded the lock with her body and tapped in the code. And she said that she changed the code regularly. I would have to do the same later. I would have to do everything the way that she did it.

She took the boxes of jewellery and gold coins out of the safe deposit compartment one by one. She removed the lids of the boxes and showed me the contents, as if I had never seen them before. I knew where and when my father had bought every jewel and how much it had cost. Sometimes she tried on a pair of earrings and inspected herself in the mirror of her powder compact, or she put on a gold bracelet and surveyed the effect. Even in her darkest periods, when she felt too bad to go to work, she never missed the visits to her safe deposit box. For her it was meat and drink.

For every family party we went to the bank to choose the jewellery with which my mother would adorn herself. First I had to help my mother decide the outfit she would wear, a suit, or a dress, or a skirt and blouse, and if so which blouse? Was it an occasion for silk, or rather cotton, or perhaps linen? Should she go for cotton and a silk scarf? Twice silk was perhaps overdoing it. Her sister was coming too and she would get jealous when she saw all that silk and the day would be ruined, or the evening. On the other hand she couldn't always go on indulging her sister. She had to be able to live her own life, like her sister did. So yes, perhaps the silk blouse after all. The yellow or the white?

The white, I said. I usually said the white. She then chose the yellow. When I said the yellow, she decided to wear the white.

'This is wild silk,' she said. 'Feel.'

I felt.

My mother couldn't understand how some women could wear synthetic fabrics. She couldn't stand them on her skin. 'Silk is best,' she said. 'Wild silk.'

With great satisfaction she hung the clothes she was going to wear ready in the bathroom. She put on her reading glasses, checked that there were no stains anywhere, that all the buttons were sewn on properly and especially that no seams were loose, and proceeded to the next step: considering matching jewellery, jewellery that would command respect, without falling into excess. Excess must be avoided. Excess was vulgar. If my mother wore something with a low-cut neckline, she almost always chose her pearl necklace, which she had been given by my father on my birth. But sometimes it occurred to her that she might be too old for a décolleté and definitely did not want to give the impression of being on the lookout for a man. Then we went to the bank again. 'We can go as often as we like,' said my mother. 'We pay a rental for our safe deposit box.'

When Gilles was born, she opened a savings book for him with five thousand francs in it. Every birthday and every New Year an amount was added to it, but he would only have access to the money when he was grown-up. She saved it for him. She put his savings book in the safe deposit box too, but by then our outings to the safe depository had long since come to an end. She would no longer have trusted me. She was terrified that M would follow her to the bank and try to force his way into the depository. In all honesty I was frightened of that too. At the same time I often considered it myself. The thought of the gold and diamonds in my mother's safe deposit box made me ill with frustration. M was right: wealth was unjustly distributed. There was enough for everyone but the rich hoarded it away, so the poor had to grab it from them. Why did she give so little money to me, her only child? It was my inheritance. She owed it all to my father. I was his child.

If I had not needed it, she would have given it to me. Then I would have deserved it. Now I did need it, badly in fact, I had no right to it. Jérôme and Elise were not given a savings book, since I had shamed her by marrying a prisoner and by landing in jail myself because of complicity in sex crimes committed by the prisoner. I had forced her to come and visit me in prison.

That was *me*, Mummy! My children were not complicit!

Devil's brood, that's what she called them. And she said she was ashamed to go out in the street, as she could feel people's eyes boring into her back.

'Don't you know what to do not to have children? How many more children of that man's are you going to bring into the world? If your father were still alive, he would drag you away from him! He wouldn't rest until he had got you away from there.'

They were my children too, Mummy, and your grandchildren.

When I went to ask her for money, she stood for a wretchedly long time with that big purse in her hands before she unclipped it. Usually she started talking about the neighbour's daughter, who was married to a surgeon. He worked in a private hospital in Cairo where only the very best surgeons were allowed to perform operations. The couple lived in a house with a swimming pool and maids and servants, and they had a house on the coast too, since Cairo was unbearably hot in summer. In both houses there was a room for the mother, who spent long, carefree weeks there. Some mothers, my mother said, had struck lucky with their sons-in-law.

Sometimes in the course of her story she put the purse back in her handbag as if she could no longer remember why she had taken it out. Then I had to ask her again if I could please have money for Pampers and milk powder and wet wipes and ointment to rub on their bottoms, things that M thought were superfluous and for which he definitely wouldn't cough up any money. He wasn't stupid. My mother could have transferred the money, but no, each time I had to go and ask her for it in her villa in Waterloo. I had to get together money for petrol, I had to ensure that the children looked their best, and I had to drive for almost an hour to Waterloo. Each time I had to thank her, each time she said that the children looked awful, and I also looked a state. 'What have you done to your hair? You're covered in spots. You've put on weight. You've lost weight. Are you taking your medication? There's a stain on your skirt. Gilles' trousers are too short. Jérôme needs shoes. The child wants to walk. Can't you see that? He's cross-eyed. Is he cross-eyed? When are you going to clean your car? You need new tyres. I don't want you to park your dirty car in front of my house. Have you heard anything from him? Don't tell me. I don't want to know.'

She said: 'As long as you come to ask for money, I know you're not stealing it from me. Or else you would have to be very devious. Even more devious than I think you are. It's terrible, isn't it, that a mother has to say that about her daughter.'

I had lost the plot and I was plotting. 'Sleep with the dog and you catch its fleas.' She had discussed it with her bank manager. He had said that these things were wont to happen. 'We live in strange times,' he had said. 'Your daughter has been exposed to malign influences. Fortunately she has had a good upbringing. Hopefully that will provide the much needed counterbalance.'

'Why don't you marry the bank manager? You'd make a lovely couple. You could spend your wedding night in the depository, adorned with all your jewels.'

I burst out laughing. I must tell M, I thought. It will make him laugh too.

'Impertinence will get you nowhere, Odette. How can you talk like that in the presence of your children?'

'They're used to worse than that, Mummy.'

'I expect they are.'

And she reminded me that I had embraced my unhappiness with my eyes wide open. She had warned me.

'But you wouldn't listen.'

I wanted to get away from you, Mummy. I was sick of your fleas.

Out of the frying pan into the fire.

'You're nothing, you're a zero, you're a rag. Without me you'd be nothing. Without me you'd still be sleeping with your mother every night. Who would have wanted you if I hadn't taken pity on you? I saved you.'

The words of the most hated man in Belgium to the most hated woman. When he felt provoked, when he felt I was challenging him. When I put his patience to the test, tried to drive him into a corner. And did I appreciate all he did for me? For me and my children. A normal wife would be grateful.

He put his hands on my shoulders and pushed, pushed until I was on my knees.

'Your mother was right. You should have died in that accident, your father should have survived.'

'I'm sorry, M.'

'You're not sorry.'

'I'm sorry, I'm really sorry.'

'How can I believe that? I wish I could, but you make it impossible for me.'

'I'm sorry, I'm sorry, I'm sorry.' Repeated endlessly.

And I really was sorry. I was sorry since the accident that *I* had survived, and my father hadn't. Everything would have been better if I had died then. I was sorry that I didn't take the bus to school, like the girl next door, who was now married to a surgeon. Perhaps I would have married a surgeon too if I had taken the school bus back then. I had never asked my father to take me to school, but I was still very sorry he had driven me. I was the cause of his death. I was a murderess.

It was even worse for my mother. I reminded her every hour of the day of the precious husband she had lost. I was responsible for the accident *and* I was all she had left. She had to love what she abhorred. She clung to me, while she hated me.

'Don't dare leave me.'

For years and years I didn't dare. And I hated her and loved her. She was all I had, my darling, darling Mummy.

For all that time, all those years she was loyal to me, however deeply she was ashamed. She was the only one I could turn to, who I was a hundred per cent sure would never leave me in the lurch. Even when I was in prison and brought shame on her, I could depend on her. And she knew she could depend on me. When she needed me I was there for her. Or I tried to be there for her. At the end when she was so ill, I arranged lots of things for her. From prison. It cost a bomb in telephone calls. She was grateful to me for that. 'Thank you, pet,' she wrote, 'for looking after your little Mummy so well.' *Ta pauvre petite maman chérie.*

How I would have liked to make her happy! It eats away at me that I didn't make her happy. She suffered so badly and I made her suffering worse.

'Pray,' says Sister Virginie. 'Your mother is in heaven. She will hear you.'

If only I had that calm confidence! My faith is so poor. Poor sinner that I am. Great sinner.

I deserve Elise to break my heart, like I broke my mother's. Please don't let Elise break my heart. Don't let her fall into the clutches of a man like her father.

Mummy, who art in heaven, watch over your grandchildren. And forgive me, forgive me, forgive me.

Why did you make it so difficult for me?

You made it impossible for me.

And look where I am now.

Nowhere.

Don't cry, Odette. No self-pity. Anouk disapproves of self-pity, so we can't afford it.

Anouk would say: you are somewhere, Odette. You are where you want to be.

One thing is certain: I'm no longer in hell. I have left hell behind.

When I first told my mother about M, she didn't believe me. She couldn't believe that a man wanted me. And if he wanted me, she couldn't believe that I would move in with him. Was that what she had sacrificed her life for me for?

'He's married,' I said to needle her. 'He has a wife and two sons.'

She began screaming. 'Say it's not true. Please say it's not true.'

I said it was true.

She made me kneel in front of Daddy's photo and handkerchief. 'Say it to him. If you dare say it to him, you have no shame. You are lost. And so am I.'

She had just come back from the hairdresser's. She had had her hair put up in a beehive. She looked like a sailing ship that was decked out to sail into harbour where a welcome committee of dignitaries stood in attendance. And a brass band. In her despair she grabbed her hair and tried to pull it out. In a tantrum she destroyed the hairdresser's work, and threw herself on the ground.

My mother was proud of the fact that she had had no other man since my father's death. I was her witness that she had never shared her bed with another man, as I slept in her bed every night. She used me to keep her reputation untarnished, to prove she had cobwebs between her legs. That is how M put it: your mother has cobwebs between her legs. She had no candle on her bedside table. I really think her cunt had closed up, or had been sealed, cauterised by her gynaecologist. That was the difference between her and me. I did have a cunt, and I had to feed it with sperm. My cunt was hungry. It must be hungry, since otherwise Gilles, Jérôme and Elise would never have been born. Sister Virginie tells me I mustn't feel guilty about that. God wants us to reproduce. He gives us a helping hand. 'What woman would be prepared to be pregnant for nine months *and* to give birth if she didn't desire a man? God has arranged it splendidly.'

'Jehovah is almighty,' I said.

She nodded. I didn't dare ask her if she knows that hunger too, or knew it.

Help me, God, help me. And have pity on Your poor sinner.

It would have been better. It would definitely have been better.

No use crying over spilt milk.

If I could turn back the clock. Be six years old again. Wake up on the day of the accident. Say to my Daddy: 'Daddy, today I'm going to school on the bus.'

Calm down, Odette. You must learn to be calm.

Breathe in deeply, and breathe out. Don't forget to breathe out.

She never left the house without gloves, or a scarf. Every Sunday and every Wednesday she and I visited my father's grave. We cleaned it. We stood there with our eyes closed and heads bowed. We said a Hail Mary, a Lord's Prayer. We stood there.

She didn't do it for him, but for herself, for her spotless reputation.

When I'm dead I don't want a grave. I don't want my children to stand at my grave. They must live, play in the sun.

I don't know for how long she had hoped to use me. I was twenty-one. My father had been killed fifteen years before. He had caused the accident. He had let go of the steering wheel in order to hunt for cigarettes in his trouser pocket. He never smoked when I was in the car with him, but he always stuck a cigarette between his lips, so that he could light up as soon as he had dropped me off at school.

He was always her last resort. If I wanted to sleep over at a friend's, I had to kneel in front of his photo and tell him I chose a friend over my mother. If I wore a blouse that she thought was too sexy, I had to tell my father that I wanted to go into the street like a whore. On that day when I first told my mother about M, he was once again called in as referee. I knelt in front of his photo and said: 'Daddy, dear Daddy, you don't have to worry about me anymore. I've met the man of my life. He will look after me now. He will look after me like a father, a brother, a friend, a husband. I'm happy, Daddy. For the first time in all these years I'm happy. I'm so happy that I have to control myself not to burst out laughing and singing. He can do anything he likes with me, Daddy. I'm his. The more I'm his, the...'

She had hit me. Straight in the face. The blood spurted from my lip. It was a good preparation for what was to follow, but I wasn't to know that. I thought I was leaving behind everything that was bad in my life.

She was shocked by what she had done. She tried to put her arms round me. I pushed her away. '*You* should have bled to death in that wreck,' I said. 'You, not him should have taken me to school. Daddy and I would have been happy without you!'

Saying that was better than sex. I ran my hand across my lips and wiped my bloody hand on her white carpet. There was nothing I wouldn't have dared do on that day. It's because of his sperm, I thought. He shoots it into me and makes me strong.

I don't know what she did with the carpet. Whenever I went to her place, I looked to see if I could find it anywhere. When M was in prison and I and the children sometimes moved in with her for a week, I couldn't find it anywhere. When I asked about it, she couldn't remember what I was talking about. Sometimes she asked who I was, and what those children were doing in her house. At first I thought it was a game, playacting. I thought she was trying to provoke. Later, when she really had dementia, everyone said that she forced herself to lose her mind. But no, Anouk says, that's not how it works.

It seems that they cut her hair very short in the care home. It's easier for nursing. I would have liked to see her with a short haircut like that. Gilles says it made her younger. Younger and gentler. He went to her funeral. There weren't many people.

You were proved right, Mummy.

First he saved me, and then he made me the most hated woman in Belgium.

'No,' Anouk says, 'you did that yourself.'

I have omitted nothing. I have told the full story. I have racked my memory so as not to skip any details. I was aware I had to tell the truth. That is very important for the next-of-kin of the victims. My mother wanted to know every single detail about the accident. Again and again I had to tell her everything I remembered. She was in regular touch with the witness. He told her for the umpteenth time exactly what he had seen. And so I also did my best to be as complete as possible, at first with her, later with the examining magistrates and the judges and the psychologists and the psychiatrists and the lawyers and the warders and the whole army of people who wanted to sound me out, give me a grilling, squeeze me dry like a lemon.

But they wanted to hear different things. They were never satisfied.

They wouldn't see that I was a victim, and still am.

If I had said what they hoped to hear, I would have had to lie.

And I didn't want to lie.

There were no commissioning clients, or any networks. There was no protection from above. I would have loved it if we had had protection. Alas. There was only M, and pals of his who were under his thumb because they were addicted to some substance or other that he could provide. And there was me, his slave.

Was I his slave?

'She is a clever woman, calculating and sharp. From her first day in prison she has carefully planned her release.'

I look at the words in the paper, as I look at my photo. Is that me?

I would like to be like that: calculating and sharp.

Then I would never have fallen for M.

There was a guy who studied with me, and had a thing for me. At his house on Twelfth Night he made sure I got the piece of cake with the bean in it and so became king, or rather queen. I still have photos of me with a paper crown on my head and his arm round my shoulder. Everyone said he was in love with me. Perhaps he was, but he never declared his love to me, not even that evening when I wore the crown and he put his arm round my shoulder and I let my head rest on his shoulder. Everyone expected it would happen, and I expected it too and perhaps I would have said yes, you're my king, I'm you're queen, but he didn't ask anything. Perhaps he felt intuitively that I am a bad and sinful person. *Ayez pitié, ayez pitié.*

When I was in prison for the first time, he rang me, but I refused to come to the telephone. What was I supposed to say to him?

Sister Virginie says: 'People sometimes forget that we all have to die. We don't know when.'

Suppose a murderer is a workman of God's, that God has decided that the time has come for x or y, and that the murderer must ensure that the job is done. He is sent forth by God. In that case the murderer is in a certain sense guiltless. He or she is like wax in God's hand. He is a follower, an executor, an instrument.

I spend too much time alone. It isn't good for a person to be alone so much. The thoughts you have then!

Now and in the hour of our death.

Geneviève Lhermitte was alone a lot too. That can lead to dramas.

You're not alone, says Sister Virginie. You are with God.

I wish I felt it. I really do.

Someone has made a film about Lhermitte. *À perdre la raison*. Our Children: Loving Without Reason. Her husband—ex-husband—and the doctor who lived with them in the house he had bought for them, that doctor bought everything for them, paid all the bills, that wasn't normal—well, that doctor and the ex-husband tried to stop the film, but failed. Different names were used in the film and so they couldn't do anything.

Any resemblance to actual facts and actual people is purely coincidental.

Yes, yes.

M would say: you never had any mind, so how could you lose it?

He would say it three or four times in succession. And if one of his pals was there, he would nudge them and then they would both laugh their heads off.

Hahaha.

Don't react. Don't get angry. And certainly don't cry, as I did the first time he riled me with that ABBA song. Very soon after I met him, I sang it for him. 'Waterloo! Napoleon did surrender.' I could sing the whole song. I still can for that matter. Everyone in Waterloo could sing it. I was fourteen when ABBA won the Eurovision Song Festival. We dressed up like ABBA, we danced like ABBA, we sang like them. We had won that festival too.

It's best not to tell M something like that. All he can think of is that he was not there. 'That hurts. Here.' He placed his hand on his chest. And I felt sorry for him. I felt guilty. I thought I had hurt him.

Hurt M!

Even my mother liked ABBA. Everyone in Waterloo liked them. Signatures were collected to offer them the freedom of the town, and to get them to perform in Waterloo.

Dream on.

Actually they're cows and arrogant bastards. Why couldn't they come to Waterloo? They use our name, yes, but a 'thank you' was too much trouble.

'Waterloo! Promise to love you for ever more.'

Did he ever say that? I'll always love you, Odette?

I'll look after you. *That*'s what he said.

If I did as he said, he would look after me. 'Forget your mother. Forget everything you've ever known. You have no parents. Neither have I. We were born without parents. I'm your father, your mother, your husband, your brother, your grandparents. You were born today. Like me. We are twins, monozygotic twins.'

I don't regret anything. That is hell, real hell, knowing that I would do it again, would do everything again.

'Men are selfish. Some men.' And then with a laugh: 'Most men.'

Says Anouk. Who else?

She has seen that film about Lhermitte. 'A heavy film. Very heavy, even though the murders aren't shown. Or the corpses. You can't show those things.'

Did I nod? I don't remember.

Why can't the corpses be shown?

When a woman murders five children there are five corpses.

I hate that hypocrisy.

In the film she had only four children, and they are younger than Lhermitte's. You have to know what happened, otherwise you don't understand the film properly. And the actress playing Lhermitte is much prettier than Lhermitte. Especially at the beginning of the film when she has just met her husband. In the end she is a neurotic wreck. A madwoman.

If I were to make a film like that, every detail would have to be right, and clear.

Five corpses are five corpses.

Beautiful is beautiful; ugly is ugly.

I would ask Lhermitte: did you thrust or cut? She would have to demonstrate it to the actress. And she would have to explain what she did with the blood. I would demand the same accuracy as the court in a judicial reconstruction. Why else do you make such a film?

Sometimes my interest in Lhermitte is pathological, at other times Anouk herself can't stop talking about her.

That woman had to deal with everything on her own. If something went wrong she got the blame. In the long run she apologised for things she had not done. When she murdered her children she had stopped teaching. She no longer had the energy. She had to take pills, but they didn't help, or not enough.

We know about that, pills that don't work but that you have to pay for. Diseases that leave doctors perplexed.

'Isn't that remarkable,' Anouk says, 'that both of you were teachers?'

I don't react, it's best not to react, it's safest. I must keep silent for the rest of my life.

If I ever get out of here, I can buy or rent the film, because the chance of it being shown in prison is zero. And I can also go and visit the woman. Perhaps they won't give me permission. Most probably they won't give me permission.

Bastards.

Prejudiced. Narrow-minded. Perverted, but still they have an instant judgement on everything and everyone. At the Day of Judgement they will be affrighted, but it will be too late. Then there will be gnashing of teeth, and deafening lamentation. 'Everything in this country is rotten,' M said. 'Rotten to the core. You have to live as an anarchist here; otherwise you are an accessory to the corruption and rottenness. You can't rely on anyone. You have to do everything yourself. They finished my father off, and they tried to finish me off. I can't let that happen and I won't let them finish you off either. I wasn't able to help my younger brother. He destroyed himself. Stupid, stupid, stupid. You mustn't destroy yourself, Odette. Promise me you will never destroy yourself. You must wipe *them* out, like parasites. They are the evil, not us. Do you understand me? Tell me you understand me.'

It won't be much longer, my lawyer says.

They're trying to stop it. They are going through the legal literature with a fine-tooth comb in the hope of finding something to stop my release. And they are whipping people up. Total strangers take to the streets. They lodge complaints, and make a lot of noise, although they know nothing. They are naïve children. You can't blame them for anything, anything at all. Meanwhile the magistrates are leaving no stone unturned. 'Let them go on looking,' my lawyer says. 'They won't find anything. We didn't make any mistakes.'

He talks like M used to talk, without doubt or hesitation.

He's not doing it for me, he says, but for the country, the country that has laws, laws that must be respected, otherwise there will be no more civilisation.

And do I know where the system of justice originated?

I shake my head.

'When you're released,' he says, 'you should look it up, on the internet.'

And I shall also look up my house on the internet, I think. I will look up everything and everybody on the internet, so I know they exist.

I dare to look him in the eye. Not for long, but I do dare.

He said that I must trust him, that he would do everything he could, provided I trusted him.

'It's better if you tell me everything. You can also write it down, if you find that easier.'

Some things can't be put into words. And if they can, they don't descend into my mouth or into my pen. They are in my head, but they stay suspended there. I can't even summon up the words to explain that.

8

'A weak personality, easily manipulated, a tormented woman.' That's what my lawyer said about me in an interview. 'My counsel' they called him in the paper. Alain, Elise says. Mr Moyson, I say. He receives hate mail because he is defending me. People describe what they would like to do to him, or to his children, which he fortunately doesn't have.

To me he says: 'You're a strong woman. You have survived M and you will survive this too. He will never be released. You will. You've met all the conditions.'

The conditions are: accommodation, work and acceptance of therapy. Anouk will take charge of condition three. And thanks to my guardian angel, my Sister Virginie, the convent of Malonne will meet conditions one and two. She has won them all over and convinced them that they must give me a chance. Not only me, but God too, since through me God can display his heavenly goodness and phenomenal strength, like a peacock fanning its tail. I am a tool in his hands, an instrument.

'Eleven elderly nuns offer murderess refuge.' They

write 'elderly', but they mean 'gaga'. The walls of their convent have been daubed with my initials, and with that word: murderess.

Lhermitte is the murderess, a fivefold murderess.

Malonne has already had to fork out forty-two thousand euros on security. That is one million six hundred and eighty thousand Belgian francs, more than M paid for the hovel in which he made me and the children live, the hovel that so shocked Anouk when she peeped at it on the internet. She should have seen the inside, and then she really would have been shocked. We didn't have a bathroom, did we Anouk? We washed at the sink in the kitchen. And then I had to nag at M for ages to please fit a geyser. And he also put in an electric heater, which cost a fortune to run. He couldn't care less, since I had to pay the bill, otherwise that heater would never have been installed. He didn't care either that the fuse blew when I used the iron while the heater was on. I was supposed to switch it off first, but sometimes I forgot, since my head was pounding from morning till night, even when I had taken the medication prescribed by the doctor, which M said was useless, and maybe he was right, because it didn't help, even though the doctor maintained that it *did* help. I must be patient, and give the medication time to work, and I must rest.

Yes, yes.

'You've got yourself really good quarters here,' said M when he dropped by, unexpectedly, always unexpectedly, as if he was hoping to catch me with a lover. What lover would want to set foot in that hovel?

He pulled open the fridge. 'Isn't there any food in the house?' A wife must have food in the house for her husband.' And he said that he had his eye on a larger fridge, one with a freezer compartment, and he would bring it if I liked. 'See how well I look after you lot.' His lordship was in a good mood and brimming with energy. His lordship had been released from prison and the problems that had plagued him had been solved. They had melted away like snow in the sun. The traces were buried deep in the earth. The remnants. No one could see them. Eyes closed and traps shut.

Without a doubt the new problems, which would do for him *and* me, were already in the making at that time, but there was no crystal ball in my house in which we could have seen it. If there had been one, he would probably have refused to look. He would have smashed it.

Elise coughed in her sleep, a raw, rasping cough, which the nurse from *Enfance et Famille* said we should keep an eye on. 'Keep an eye on it or keep an ear open?' was my reaction. 'Both,' he replied with a mischievous laugh, and for a moment, for a moment I'd hoped that he... Oh, who would have wanted me, an invalid, a neurotic drudge with three children, and a husband who taunted her to death?

Jérôme stood staring at his father with a bubble of snot at the end of his nose. 'Give Daddy a kiss, Jérôme. Say: thank you, Daddy.' Gilles had crawled away under the table. Brutus and Nero were sitting there too, while they should have been outside in the yard, behind the gate guarding what in M's eyes needed guarding. I couldn't let the children play among those wrecks, but Gilles was fascinated by them. He wanted to be a mechanic, like his Daddy. He wanted to know how you could reclaim and repair car parts, and sell them for money, lots of money.

'Daddy isn't a mechanic, he's an electrician.'

An electrician who makes his wife and children live in a hovel under the constant threat of a short circuit. The whole house needed rewiring and all the fuses needed replacing, but M didn't think it was necessary, since he and his brothers had lived in a much worse slum with their mother. There was mould on the walls, but he hadn't complained. He had done what had to be done. The nights in that house had wrecked his lungs.

'Do you want to wreck my lungs too, and the children's? Will you be happy then?'

'I want them to feel what I felt, and I want *you* to feel what I felt, while you were asleep in a villa in Waterloo!'

'But you don't feel anything. You're always complaining that you don't feel anything!'

Bam, a blow in my face, and another. And then his hand tearing off my bra, his panting in my ears. 'Not here, M, not where the children are watching...'

'So can't they see how they were made?'

They would have done better to give those forty-two thousand euros to the victims, the victims that the papers are full of once again and whose names everyone in the country can recite.

Me too.

I have no money for them. All my money is for my children. They need it. No one will help them if I don't.

Someone who has money is in a strong position and has nothing to fear from anyone, including her husband.

'Someone who prays is in a strong position, Odette, and has nothing to fear from anyone,' says Sister Virginie, correcting me.

She's right, she's always right. But even in prison life is unsustainable without money. Here too you need money for everything, for stamps, for telephone cards, for paper, for shampoo, for the television rental, for extra milk, for the occasional piece of chocolate or a bit of fruit, or a waffle or a piece of cheese. At the beginning I was in dire straits. They had blocked my bank account. That was the first thing they did when they locked me up here. They blocked my account *and* they made sure my benefits were stopped, although I had been certified as an invalid and was entitled to those benefits. I still am. They even demanded that I repay all the benefits I had ever received, since I had worked for M, they said. I was not entitled to benefits, as I had been his accomplice, his right hand. I thought I was going mad. Meanwhile I had to pay an old phone bill. With what money? And so I found myself begging Mummy please to send some money, as I couldn't work, the other prisoners did not want me to and the warders could not guarantee my safety. The women here would have scratched my eyes out. They spat in my face, they pulled my hair, they pinched me. A warder threatened to starve me. There I was. Like Daniel in the lion's den. Like Job on his dunghill. Mummy simply didn't seem to understand that I needed money and that she was the only one I could ask. She had to send me money, since there was also my lawyer, who had to be paid. Without a lawyer I didn't have a chance. He was my only chance, the straw to which I clung. That was an expensive business. It still is an expensive business; very, very expensive.

I don't know how I would have managed to pay it all without Mummy's bequest, which thank God I was able to channel to the children. Thank you, smart solicitor, who fixed that for me, so that my children have been able to pay my bills down to the present. What a Calvary!

And I thank you, dear sisters of Malonne, who refused to be blackmailed. However loud the shouting outside the convent gates, it makes no impact on them.

Bravo!

'We're not afraid,' says Sister Virginie. 'God is with us. He supports us with advice and practical help. And he gives us strength. We do nothing without listening to Him.'

Yesterday she and I read the Psalms together again. And Matthew 7. 'Ask, and it shall be given you; seek, and ye shall find; knock, and it shall be opened unto you.'

I ask one thing: a new chance. For years and years I have begged for a new chance. So I can finally live, for the first time.

When I am released, says the mayor, Malonne will have to employ thirty extra police officers to protect me and the nuns. The municipality cannot pay for those police officers; the federal government will have to do it.

They find money then.

There's always money, said M. Money is a detail. And he told me not to come nagging about money. If I needed some, I must make sure I found it. He had already spent far too much money on me and my children. He shouldn't have got married to me. He should have looked for a woman with money, a rich widow like my mother. I was a bottomless pit, a pitiless bottom. Oh, how witty and amusing we are again.

That father of one of the murdered girls, the one who always had the most to say, went to see the nuns with his wife. His photo was in all the papers again. He has aged, but I recognised him at once. He had brought a thick pile of documents to make it clear to the nuns that they are dealing with a psychopath. The nuns didn't realise, he said. They are old, unworldly women. He hoped that they would finally open their eyes to the truth. They must also think of their own safety, he said. Do they really want to live under the same roof with a compulsive psychopath like me?

And that photo of me handcuffed and with a bullet-proof vest crops up everywhere. I spent a long time looking at the woman in the photo. I wondered what I would think of her if I were not that woman. She looks furtive, as if she has something to hide. The longer I looked at her, the more she started to look like Lhermitte, as if she and I are one and the same.

I too have lost my mind. I lost it years and years ago. I don't want it back. I never want to realise what happened. It didn't happen. It can't have happened. And if it did happen, someone else did it. Perhaps that madwoman Geneviève Lhermitte; she is capable of anything. And now she has lodged a complaint against the psychiatrist who treated her. He should have seen it coming. He should have had her sectioned. I didn't have a psychiatrist. I had a GP who said I should rest, and who prescribed pills that didn't help. I had no shoulder to cry on. I had my children. For them, as slippery as a snake, I have found the way I must travel in order to be free again.

Some fruits rot without ever having been ripe.

I was such a fruit.

I felt dirty when he touched me.

The dirt excited me.

It had to happen, I thought. Everything was exactly right. I was grateful to him for doing what he did. It was what I deserved.

When I thought about it, I only had to contract the muscles of my cunt a few times and I came. Sometimes I fantasised that he was pissing on me. Or he made me bend over, hoisted up my skirt, pulled down my panties and slapped cow shit on my buttocks.

I never want anyone to put his hand in my panties again.

I never want to come again.

I have no cunt.

I will be shocked, Anouk says, when I get out. People talk much more freely about sex. Sex toys and sex clubs are quite normal now. Rich gays buy eggs, pay surrogate mothers and adopt the child. The child becomes theirs, a child with two Daddies. No one makes a fuss about it. And everyone has a mobile phone, and an internet connection. People book holidays on the internet, they order tickets, they buy clothes, find a sweetheart, they sell junk they want to get rid of, they download films and music. Even at primary school all the children have mobiles.

'Children get the hang of them very quickly.'

As she says this I see in a flash the digital watch of the girl who did not want to read the clock face. I was doing my placement with the third year and had to teach the pupils to read the clock, the real clock with hands and a face. That girl was called Noémie, and she had lovely blond curls of which she was obviously very proud. She didn't need to read the clock, she said. She had been given a digital watch by her Granny. 'Look!' She walked from her place to show me it. 'It's much more practical.' Eight years old and already such a pert little thing. 'What will you do if your watch is stolen?' I asked.' Or if you lose it, of if it gets broken?'—'My

Granny will buy me a new one.'

In the placement report it said that I had disciplinary problems. I let the children walk freely round the classroom. Was I supposed to tie them to their chairs?

'I'm going to a convent,' I say to Anouk.

'The nuns are on the internet. Sister Virginie always sends an email when she comes here.'

Is she lying? Is she telling the truth?

'You don't have to look so incredulous, Odette. The nuns move with the times. I'll give you my email address when you go. Then you can send me emails from the convent. People don't ring each other so much anymore; they email or they chat.'

Chat. Again and again that magical word.

Who would I want to chat with if I could?

Not with him.

There's also something called Skype. On that you can chat *and* see the person. You need a webcam for that. People sit at their computers in their birthday suits, chatting each other up. They have sex via their computers, so avoiding pregnancies and AIDS.

Young girls now wheedle money out of paedophiles on the internet. They sit in front of their webcams and undo one button and then another, but if the man wants more he has to pay. He pays and doesn't get to see anything. They laugh at him. They threaten to go to the police. They needn't have tried that with M.

Lead us not into temptation, lead us not into temptation.

'I'm going to work,' I reply. 'And when I'm not working I shall be praying.'

'Even the nuns don't pray day and night, Odette. Sometimes they simply enjoy sitting in the sun.'

Simply enjoying sitting in the sun.

I must remember those words. What are you doing, Odette? I'm simply enjoying sitting in the sun.

When Gilles comes and visits me in the convent, I can ask him if I can use his iPad. He hasn't said anything to me about it, nor has he promised me he will visit me more often in the convent than here. I know I mustn't raise the subject. I must respect his privacy. Most probably he will say something spontaneously if I don't ask him. I haven't brought up his girlfriend either yet. I pretend I don't read those interviews, as if I don't know he gives them.

'They don't like you asking questions because they are frightened of not knowing the answer,' Anouk says. 'They'd rather drop dead than admit that.'

By 'they' she means: men. Beings who at all times must defend their honour. Their ego and their honour, which are located in their penis, in their scrotum, with hair growing on it.

My father liked nothing better than for me to ask him questions.

'Come on,' he would goad me, 'ask me another question.'

And how delighted he was when he didn't know the answer: he had something else to look up. 'There's no such thing as a stupid question,' he said. 'Or stupid people. The only stupid people are people who don't dare ask questions.'

In that case your daughter has become very very stupid, Daddy. All that effort for nothing.

When my mother's house was cleared my father's encyclopaedia was no longer there, nor did they find the children's encyclopaedia he had bought for me. I should have liked to have it in here with me. Perhaps my mother threw it away, or put it out with the waste paper. Books brought dust into the house, she said. My father had to put his books in the garage. The last time I visited, they were still there.

Publishers cannot sell their encyclopaedias and dictionaries for love nor money, says Anouk, now there is Wikipedia. I will be able to pick up a second-hand encyclopaedia on eBay.

Gilles is in the paper again, with a photo and an interview. He has turned into a handsome young guy, better-looking than his father, and me. He is not ashamed of his background, he says. He doesn't care who knows who he is. He has been given another name, but he doesn't hide behind it. That other name cost a lot of money, but he threw it away. Brave Gilles, who looked after his little brother and sister when his Mummy was arrested right in front of him; who when I was finally allowed to call him from prison asked if it was true what the journalists were saying about me and his father. Journalists have no sense. You should know better than tell things like that to a child.

However deeply I am ashamed, I am proud of him. I am proud of his pride. And I am proud of the other two as well.

They don't appear in the media.

It's better that way.

Gilles makes too much noise. He thinks they can't touch him. That's what his father thought. Even after we had landed in jail the first time because of his stupid actions, he kept saying: everything is under control, and that I mustn't keep nagging. Even when I hadn't said anything, he thought I was nagging. I looked as if I was about to start nagging, to wind him up.

The famous mechanism with which I wound him up every five minutes, or Gilles wound him up.

'Don't start,' he said. Because he had stomach ache from the worthless food I served up to him. A dog wouldn't have eaten it.

People with stomach trouble have difficult characters. They have stomach problems because they have a trying temperament and stomach pain makes their nature still more trying. I often told him that he should see the doctor about his stomach, but he didn't want to. He said I cooked the wrong things. Before he knew me he never had stomach problems. No one in his family had stomach trouble. They were all good eaters and digesters. It was with me, he said, that all the misery had begun. I had brought him bad luck.

Always playing the blaming game.

At every birthday of Gilles' he had a stomach crisis. He resented his own son being in the limelight. He had to be the centre of attention. Jealous of a child. He had never grown up himself and so was jealous of a child. If I happened to mention I was tired, his reaction was: 'Have you any idea how tired I am?'

Gilles in the paper: 'My mother did nothing wrong by transferring her mother's inheritance to our names and ensuring that our handful of childhood memories is not taken away from us.'

That's right, my boy. Which doesn't mean that you should trumpet it about. Everything you say will be used against you, and then against me, your poor mother. I am accused of 'fraudulent insolvency': pretending to be poorer than I am to avoid paying compensation to the victims.

And what about my children? Is my principal duty

not to care for my own children? 'Or what man is there of you, whom if his son ask bread, will he give him a stone? Or if he ask a fish, will he give him a serpent.' Matthew 7. And there follows: 'Therefore all things whatsoever ye would that men should do to you, do ye even so to them: for this is the law and the prophets.' On that point I fell woefully short. I should have brought the children food. Dogs or no dogs, headache or no headache, fear or no fear, I should have treated them like my own children, my own flesh and blood. I shall have to do penance for the rest of my life for that. *I* shall have to do penance for that, not my children.

Mea culpa, mea culpa, mea maxima culpa.

Those children were doomed. He would have murdered them, just as he murdered those two other girls. Not murdered, but let them die. 'Let them go.' They were no longer girls, those two, but young women, M said. They could already have children.

He could have used them to breed fresh children. Then he wouldn't have to abduct any more.

They tried to escape across the roof. One of the two went over the roofs in her birthday suit. She didn't get far.

They write so much.

But it was her father who went and made a fuss at the convent, with a very self-important face and a cartload of documents and a pack of press-photographers and reporters.

'We gave him plenty of time to say what he had to say,' says Sister Virginie. 'We listened attentively. And we invited him to prayers. His wife prayed with us. He didn't.'

They gave him a jar of home-made strawberry jam,

and brochures on the retreats they organise.

He wasn't pleased.

'Don't call me a victim,' Gilles says in every interview. 'I'm not a victim.'

Who do you owe that to, lad? Who ensured that you are not left empty-handed? Your mother, who always took responsibility. And who cannot take on the responsibility for the victims as well, just as back then I could not take on the care of the children in the cellar.

Try explaining that.

They would do better to examine their own conscience and ask themselves the question: am I free of sin?

'Why beholdest thou the mote that is in thy brother's eye, but considerest not the beam that is in thine own eye?' Matthew 7. I know that whole chapter by heart.

Gilles says he had a hard time for the first few years after he left the home. He lived rough and was in with a bad crowd. Now he is on the right path. *Dieu merci.* He has bought a house together with his girlfriend. They are doing it up, with money from the inheritance, I assume. And he is looking for work. He and his girlfriend want children. 'If we have the money to support them.' That is very sensible, lad. Children can't live on air. No one can live on air.

His girlfriend knows who he is. He has told her everything. Everyone will know who he is, now he has his picture in the paper every five minutes. Does he really think they will employ him when they know who he is?

Gilles sometimes witnessed things... I tried to protect him, but he followed his father around like a puppy.

And how he chattered, his little mouth was never still. 'Shush, Gilles, Daddy is tired!'

It was always my fear that M would lose his temper and hit him, or lock him up in the cellar, the cellar I helped build, as I read in the paper, so I expect it's true.

Getting the cellar ready cost money. And time. Lots of time.

He started on things without thinking things through. He maintained that he thought things through, but he didn't.

When my children sense the evil in themselves, they must pray. Kneel on the ground and pray. First the Hail Mary, then the Lord's Prayer, then the Hail Mary again and so on. Jérôme, Elise and I have often prayed together here, without much enthusiasm, but still they did it. I never managed to persuade Gilles. Stubborn as a mule, like his father.

The children had to pray to drive out fear, fear which like a monster… I am not the monster. Fear is the monster. I could not defeat it. No one could have defeated it.

'Be sober, be vigilant; because your adversary the devil, as a roaring lion, walketh about, seeking whom he may devour.' Peter 5:8.

Am I that prey? Are my children the prey?

Protect me, God. Hold me firmly in Your hand, me and my children, so that Your enemy does not find us.

The monster sucks out your brain, like someone sucks out an egg. Greedily, slurping. And then it lets out a burp.

You can't think anymore. You want it to stop. The fear must stop.

The papers write that all that praying is playacting. And they call me a bigot. 'She'll do anything to be released.'

That's true.

Perhaps the praying began as playacting, or as a dodge, like M who served as an acolyte in prison. He maintained he had done it as a boy in the Congo. All black altar boys and him as the only white one. He still knew exactly how to do it.

Lies, nothing but lies. He was four years old when they left the Congo, driven out like vermin.

In the past I never thought of prison. 'Forest prison.' You sometimes heard of that on the news, that a revolt had broken out in Forest prison, or that a criminal had been transferred to Forest prison, or Bruges or Louvain or Nivelles, or Jamioulx, but mostly Forest, which was and remains overpopulated, and where medieval conditions prevailed. It's been like that for years and years. You heard it on the news and you didn't give it much thought. I didn't know what it was like in a prison.

Now I do.

When I am released, I shall be first transferred to Forest prison. It began on Forest ice rink and it ended in Forest prison.

Forest! Nobody ever surrendered!

They should put all the inmates in a skating rink and charge people to come and look at them, and laugh when they slip.

M wouldn't fall. He would make other people fall, like he used to in the skating rink when he did not like the look of someone's face, or if someone were skating with a girl *he* wanted to skate with, first skate with then fuck, in the caravan, always in the caravan, and always in that order, the order that had to be respected, so that everything remained under control.

I should have run away, to France. I should have buttonholed a customs man and said: take me and my children with you across the border. That was the biggest disadvantage of where I lived, said M, that it was so close to the border. The area was crawling with customs men. M drove around with red diesel in his tank, diesel intended for heating, not for cars. Customs men checked that. And they searched your boot, or your van. In that respect M had a lot of luck. A great deal of luck. Perhaps the customs men didn't feel like stopping such a wreck.

I should have said to my mother: give me some money. I should have forced her to hand over her jewels and her Krugerrands to me. 'It's crazy, Mummy, that you've got all that money, while I and the children have to live in a hovel.'

Or I should have moved in with her with the children, not for a few weeks, as I occasionally did, but for good. I should have said to her, Mummy, dear Mummy, we're coming to live with you. This is our only real home. I know that we'll get on each other's nerves and have rows, but there is no alternative. Do you remember my looking for a house or an apartment in your area that I could rent and where I could live with the children? All those houses and apartments were too expensive. I couldn't pay the rent every month. I should never have left you, Mummy. That was my big mistake. But I'm coming back and I'm not coming alone. I'm bringing my children with me, my darlings, who are your darlings too. And will you please be nice to Gilles? Will you please not let him notice that he reminds you of his father?

Or I should have tried a safe house for women. I could have asked the GP for an address. She would have known, or she would have known someone who knew.

Whatever I did, he would have found us. Even now I know he is monitored every seven minutes in his cell, I am sometimes terrified he will find me. He has escaped once, why shouldn't he escape a second time? He could disguise himself as a nun. He could send me an email and say he was coming to see me. And then I would be alone with him in my cell.

'You can tell me everything,' Anouk says. 'I understand you better than you think.'

She takes my hand and gives it a little squeeze. I know I must look in her eyes and smile.

During questioning there was a policeman who acted as if he was on my side. There was one with a wine stain below his right eye who became furious when I did not look at him and also furious when I did look at him. He pounded the table with his fist and brought his face very close to mine. I knew they wouldn't hit me. 'If they hit you,' my lawyer had said, 'we'll lodge a complaint.' It was all playacting, both the rage and the soft approach. I was used to more than that, if they were trying to impress me like that. They agree among themselves what role they will play. My lawyer had warned me. 'Don't let yourself be manipulated, or frightened. They will try everything.'

And now there is Anouk, who comes to talk to me every five minutes in her role of concerned psychotherapist, who sympathises with the inmates, because she herself was once behind bars. 'As a mother.' She believes I am good. That is because I am silent. I keep my lips tight shut. I don't bark the commands at her that I would like to: shut up. Bring me a cup of coffee. Coffee, I said. Do you call this coffee? Go and put on something else. Did you have a look in the mirror before coming here? Don't stand there gawping at me. Are you a sheep? Your breath stinks and your cunt stinks. Dozy cow.

I'd like a woman who trembles and quakes before me. Sometimes I'm nice. I fondle her breasts, I whisper sweet talk in her ear, I spoil her with presents. I say: I love you. You've got the juiciest cunt I've ever felt. I kiss her and lick her. Half an hour later I push her away. I spit in her face. I say: go and wash. I say: I don't want a whore in my bed.

So has M got into me after all?

Sister Virginie thinks that God will call me. When he calls, she says, I will hear. She prays that God will call me. For almost sixteen years she has prayed for me.

'Why?'

'It is His wish.'

That was in the very first letter she sent me, the letter that changed everything, the letter of hope. It said that God had instructed her to take care of my soul.

'The Lord often works through intermediaries. The Lord takes pity on sinners. He does not want to lose anyone, not even the greatest sinner.'

'Not even M?'

'God moves in mysterious ways.'

And she says that there is more rejoicing in heaven for one sinner who mends his ways than for the ninety-nine righteous souls who need no conversion.

'God's mercy is so great. We cannot imagine it.'

She wants me to pray for the children, not Lhermitte's, but the four whom M murdered.

Their photos are not on the wall of my cell. I don't

beg them for forgiveness. They don't exist, they never existed. They were not in that cellar. They were lies, nothing but lies. How could children survive in that small, damp space? There was no light, no air. And then there was no food either. There was no point in my going down to the cellar and opening the door. There was no one at all there, whatever M said, whatever instructions he gave me.

What father would shut up children down there?

At Gilles' school they talked about nothing else. At the school gates there were three posters with the photos of the girls. Three. And also in every shop, in every window, and on every lamppost, there were posters. The whole country was full of them. Gilles was one of the few in his class to be allowed to come to school alone on his bike. Almost all the children were brought and collected by their parents. Rosters were arranged. A psychologist came to talk to the children in every class. Someone from the police came and explained what precautions they could take. 'Don't trust anyone you don't know.'

Gilles told me about it. And he demonstrated how they had learned to defend themselves if someone tried to drag them into a van. It was a question of agility, he said, not of strength.

I asked Gilles if he was frightened of being abducted.

'Not at all, Mummy.' And he showed me his muscles.

The abductor was in prison at that point. I could have given Gilles a note to take to the headmaster with the message that everyone could sleep easy.

I thought: sooner or later Gilles will come home with a poster and ask me to hang it in the window. And I would have hung it up. What else could I have done?

The posters meant nothing. They were everywhere. Like Christmas decorations in December. I didn't listen to the radio, I didn't watch the news on television, I didn't read the newspaper. I had to think of my milk, the milk for Elise. And I had to make sure that there was food on the table for Gilles and Jérôme, that their clothes were washed and ironed, and that they went to bed on time. No one must be able to tell from looking at my children that their father was in prison, and that their mother had been in prison. I was prepared to do anything to give them as normal a childhood as possible.

I expect it's true that those girls were shut up in the cellar. Everyone says so and M has confessed. I never saw them. I didn't concern myself with them.

They were buried in the yard behind the gate of my house. He had to bury them somewhere, and he could not do it at his place. He put their corpses in grey rubbish bags and transported them like that. They weighed scarcely anything. I did not help him dig the graves. M did that alone, with a machine. He had a machine for that. He had machines for lots of things. The more machines the better. Why do the work yourself when you could have it done by a machine? I don't know what the neighbours thought about it. Perhaps they weren't home.

It was a shock when M gave me money to feed the girls in the cellar. It was a large amount, larger than I was used to receiving from him. I had gone to visit him with Elise and Jérôme. Gilles was having one of his funny moods and refused to come. When I got home I said to him that his father had given us money for a new television. I don't know why I said that.

My only wish is that my children won't have to suffer. I pray for that every day.

M did it for me. You need rest, he said. He didn't want to pay for a woman. Why should he pay for what he could grab? He didn't pay for air either, did he?

The man had such power in him.

There were times when I thought I wouldn't survive. Then he would grab me and push me against a wall, and do it while we were standing there. And each time bonk, bonk against that wall with my head, my hips, my shoulders.

Nothing would have stopped him. Nothing stopped him.

I couldn't cope by myself.

Perhaps he should have gone to a doctor. He could have given him pills to calm him down a bit. Reverse Viagra.

I hope they give him pills in prison, or camphor. I really hope so.

I couldn't give him what he needed. I tried, again and again, but it wasn't enough. It was never enough.

It got worse as time went on. They say men calm down with age, but with him it got worse.

They should pay me, he said of the women he raped. Did I realise how lucky I was to be fucked by him? There were women who flew to Africa to be fucked by a man. They had to pay. Those men asked for more and more money, and they asked for money for their families too. I got it all for nothing. And those girls he kidnapped didn't have to pay either.

They'll never admit it, but in their heart of hearts they know I'm giving them what they want. And I give you what you want too.

And then a blow with that heavy hand straight in my face, and that mocking, devilish laugh, as if he knew it turned me on. Of course he knew.

It was his foreplay.

The best thing was not to think at all, but to walk round with a blank face.

It's the best thing here too. Certainly now there's something new about me in the papers every day. They don't dare attack me anymore. They know that Anouk is protecting me. I'm her favourite. Her 'pet' they say, and you don't spit in the face of Anouk's pet. You don't lift a finger against her. But behind her back you can whisper about her for all you're worth. Do they think I'm deaf?

Will I read the book by that one girl who was rescued alive from the cellar, Anouk asks.

'Has she written a book?'

'Yes.'

'I expect it's full of lies.'

'Why do you say that?'

I shrug my shoulders. Anouk looks upset.

'Sorry,' I say. 'If you want, I'll read it.'

'If you do it, you must do it because you want to. Out of respect for her, and to confront the consequences of your actions.'

His actions, I think, not mine.

She looked beautiful at the trial. She wanted to look good, she said. That was her revenge. If she didn't look good, M would have won. And she wanted to know why he had not murdered her in that cellar. That question preoccupied her greatly.

Why should he have murdered her? He wasn't a murderer. He isn't a murderer. He did what had to be done.

If he had to murder someone, he made sure it happened. He would never have murdered anyone just like that. And when all's said and done he never murdered anyone with his own hands. He never strangled or shot anyone, or cut their throat. There were people who he had to eliminate because he had no choice. He 'let them go'. People don't understand that. There's no point in explaining.

Most people know nothing about life, nothing at all. They live under a bell jar. I lived under a bell jar too: for years and years I lived under a bell jar with Mummy. And my, the shock she had when I pulled the bell jar off and smashed it to pieces!

I think it's dreadful for those parents to have lost their children. That's the worst thing that can happen to a person. I'm a mother too, I suffer for them. Not a day goes by that I don't think of them.

I have always wanted the best for everyone, bearing in mind the words of the Gospel: 'Therefore all things whatsoever ye would that men should do to you, do ye even so to them.'

Matthew 7: 12.

Always Matthew. My counsel. My lifebuoy.

What could I have done?

What should I have done?

Outside the walls of the prison people shout that I am a whore, a murderess, a monster, a psychopath. They shout that I am worse than M. It's not him but me who is the devil, they say. And they hold up signs with the names of the girls on them, the four who died, and the two who were saved. The posters also crop up again everywhere.

'She was not the downtrodden wife,' says the father of a victim on television. 'During the trial the jury studied all the evidence carefully. The conclusion was clear: she was not a submissive wife. Not only did she hold the camera, but she gave him instructions. She told him what to do. She egged him on.'

They all deserved punishment. They were dirty and filthy. The punishment was: off with their panties, bend over and a smack on the bottom. No smacks, but thrusts of his penis in their cunt or arse. Branded and put in their place. Then his penis in their mouth. Afterwards a plaster stuck over it, and on that plaster a stamp: property of M.

In a little while when Sister Virginie comes I shall ask her to sit down. I will fill a bowl of water and put it by her feet. I will untie her shoelaces and take off her socks and shoes. I will submerge her feet in the water. I will lather them and submerge them again. I shall dry her feet with my hair. My blond angel's hair. Then I shall prostrate myself in front of her.

'Save me,' I will ask her. 'Drive the devil out of my head, my heart, my body. My body is no longer the Temple of God. The devil has captured it. He has forced his way in with his soldiers and set up camp. I did not resist strongly enough. I let him overcome my body. Drive him out. I beg you. Please.'

I shall stay lying down until I feel her wonderfully cool hand on my head and hear her voice say the words: 'Stand up, daughter. I will care for you. We will care for you.'

It is the will of God. He wants the sisters to look after me. I will cook for them and they will look after me. If the devil knocks at the door or taps on the window, they will drive him away. They will chase him away with prayers and incense. We will sing together. With my hair I will polish the tiles on which the nuns walk. Not walk, but shuffle, because oh, they are so very old. Don't die, I shall beg them. Stay alive for me, for my soul, the soul of the most hated woman in the country. Look after her!

On the Design

As book design forms an integral part of the reading experience, we would like to acknowledge the work of those who went into creating the form in which the story is housed.

Tessa van der Waals (Netherlands) is responsible for the cover design, cover typography and art direction of all World Editions books. She works in the internationally renowned tradition of Dutch Design. Her bright and powerful visual aesthetic maintains a harmony between image and typography and captures the unique atmosphere of each book. She works closely with internationally celebrated photographers, artists and letter designers. Her work has frequently been awarded prizes for Best Dutch Book Design.

Wil Westerweel is an urbex-photographer, specializing in the practice of photographing deserted buildings and structures in the urban environment. The possibility of physical danger among unstable structures and the act of 'trespassing' in forbidden places make this a high-adrenalin activity. Westerweel searches for the perfect light and angle to record 'nature taking over,' as bushes and ivy reclaim these forgotten spaces. The photo on the cover features an abandoned convent somewhere in Belgium.

The cover has been edited by lithographer Bert van der Horst of BFC Graphics (Netherlands).

Suzan Beijer (Netherlands) is responsible for the typography and careful interior book design of all World Editions titles.

The text on the inside covers and the press quotes are set in Circular, designed by Laurenz Brunner (Switzerland) and published by Swiss type foundry Lineto.

All World Editions books are set in the typeface Dolly, specifically designed for book typography. Dolly creates a warm page image perfect for an enjoyable reading experience. This typeface is designed by Underware, a European collective formed by Bas Jacobs (Netherlands), Akiem Helmling (Germany), and Sami Kortemäki (Finland). Underware are also the creators of the World Editions logo, which meets the design requirement that 'a strong shape can always be drawn with a toe in the sand.'